A KANSAS BLOODLETTING

A Kansas Bloodletting

by

Elliot Conway

Dales Large Print Books
Long Preston, North Yorkshire,
BD23 4ND, England.

British Library Cataloguing in Publication Data.

Conway, Elliot
    A Kansas bloodletting.

    A catalogue record of this book is
    available from the British Library

    ISBN   1-84262-237-4 pbk

First published in Great Britain in 1994 by Robert Hale Limited

Published in Large Print 2003 by arrangement with
Robert Hale Limited

Dales Large Print is an imprint of Library Magna Books Ltd.

Printed and bound in Great Britain by
T.J. (International) Ltd., Cornwall, PL28 8RW

Dedicated to the memory of
Norman and Terry, two bueno compadres.

ONE

Ira Brooks, slow-riding his horse along the Lexington turnpike, suddenly caught the smell of tobacco smoke and from the same direction, the thick brush on the right of the trail, the low muttering of men's voices. Instinctively Ira's hand lifted the flap of his cavalry holster belted about his middle and gripped the butt of the Colt Dragoon pistol. Then he remembered that General Robert E. Lee had signed the peace treaty at Appomattox Court House, Virginia; the war had been over these past three weeks. In those turbulent days he'd been Sergeant Ira Brooks of the 1st Kansas Mounted Volunteers, had gone through the bloody hells of Gain's Mill, Second Manassas, Chancellorsville and a dozen other equally bloody engagements not big enough to be called real battles but every bit as life risking and shit-scary.

Now he was plain Mr Ira Brooks, Kansas sodbuster, but that didn't stop him from knowing that he was riding past a well set-up ambuscade. His blood froze. He was crossing territory that used to be the stomping grounds of the brush boys, the guerillas, blue belly and reb. Those sons-of-bitches fought the war long before the politicians and the generals decided to have an official war. It looked as though some of them weren't about to end it just because the men who had started the war had upped and signed a piece of paper that said the war was over. Some of the marauders must still have old scores to settle here in the Missouri border lands.

Ira fought against the life-preserving impulse to dig his heels into his horse's ribs and hightail it along the trail to get out of rifle range of whoever it was skulking there in the brush. Then, thinking as Sergeant Ira Brooks, he opined that if the ambushers had set a trap for anyone that took their fancy he would have been dead by now. Especially if they were ex-reb mauraders, Quantrill's or Bloody Bill Anderson's boys, with him wearing a blue belly's tunic. Once round the bend in the trail Ira relaxed in the saddle, began to breathe more regularly, and allowed his horse to break into a canter.

Four riders coming along the trail towards him set his back rigid and nerves twanging apprehensively again. He drew his horse up sharply and waited for them to come up to him. Once more he tried to convince himself that the war was over: any man had the right to ride openly along any trail, turnpike or town street, without the fear of being thrown down on. But Ira admitted that the men he had heard in the brush didn't help him none in really believing one hundred per cent in what he was thinking. He only hoped that the four riders closing in on him shared the same beliefs.

They wore a mixture of well-worn reb military and civilian clothes, were armed to the back teeth with pistols in holsters belted across their bellies, and held long guns at the ready across their saddles. Ira gave them a big friendly smile. Old wary eyes set in young, hard faces, coldly looked him over as they stopped alongside him. Ira tagged them as ex-reb guerillas. Men who carried out merciless raiding and killing under the black flag of no quarter during the war were classed as renegades even by their own side. Outcasts to be shot on sight. The reason for the ambuscade became clear. Some ex-Union irregulars were aiming to get even.

Ira's cheerful, 'Howdy, gents', didn't soften the icy suspicious stares. He swallowed hard. The men he was facing didn't ponder long over the assessment of doubtful looking strangers they met before they did something about them, like pulling out their big pistols and getting rid of a possible threat to their well-being. Ira tried a more direct tack.

'I don't know whether or not it's of interest to you gents but there's a bunch of men back there in the brush on your side of the trail. The way I see it they don't figure that the war's over and they're in there hoping to bushwhack someone. Now, as I say, I don't know if you gents need to take heed of it but I thought that I'd mention it for I truly believe that the last four years have seen enough killin'. And that's the gospel truth, gents.'

Ira saw the visible relaxation in the four riders' faces as he finished speaking and his own tensions, the rigid back, the tightness in the pit of his stomach, began to unwind.

'That's real charitable, pilgrim, giving us that information, ain't it, Frank?' It was the youngest of the riders that spoke, a twitching-eyed, fuzz-chinned youth.

A man nearer Ira's age, tall, bearded, hardfaced, did the answering. 'Sure is, Jesse. We owe you mister. Sometime m'be we can repay that due if you're hankerin' to stay in this part of the territory.'

Ira touched the brim of his hat in a parting gesture. 'M'be so, gents,' he replied and kneed his horse forward. Thinking that like hell was he staying in this neck of the woods and more than likely they would only be staying around here well and truly dead.

Several miles further along the trail Ira thought he heard the distant sound of gunfire but he paid it little heed. His mind was on personal matters, such as what state his holding in the Big Creek valley, Kansas, would be in. He supposed that his nearest neighbours would be keeping their eyes on it but he also reckoned that there would be only the old men in the valley, and the few men that had returned after the war, and they would be spending their time on their own holdings, bringing them up to scratch again. It seemed that the years ahead would be anything but easy. Ira grinned thinly. None of the hundreds of men he'd seen killed during the war had died of hard work. At least he could live in peace, allowing the nightmares of the war years to fade away.

In Jackson City, Missouri, another man was

having thoughts about the Big Creek valley. Wilmore Newcombe, a thick-bellied, fleshy-faced man, dressed in a well-cut city suit, stood on the porch of the Jefferson Hotel smoking his last cigar of the day, picturing the valley in his mind's eye. Not just a section of it, but every damn acre of it, north, south, east and west.

These were momentous times. The long years of the war had stifled the growth of the country, but now it had ended it was bursting at the seams to grow. To expand in the only direction it could – westwards, crossing the last frontier. Railroad tracks were being laid across the great plains like some gigantic spider's web to carry the thousands of eager, hopeful easterners seeking to make their fortunes in the virgin territory in the postwar rebirth of the United States of America.

A man could grow big and rich if he thought big and bold and wasn't too fussy about the means he used to reach the end he wanted. Wilmore intended to be one of those up-and-coming tycoons.

He had studied the Big Creek valley real closely. Good growing land, grass enough for feeding several sizeable herds of beef. But he saw something else in the valley that could bring quicker and bigger financial gains than the ball-aching drudgery of building up a herd of cattle or walking behind a plough.

It was flat land ideal for the railroad pushing south-west. No gradients or hard rocky spurs that would require blasting or tunnelling through, causing expensive delays in the track laying that would upset the company's shareholders. Wilmore didn't doubt that the railroad surveyors would be seeing the valley the way he was seeing it – only he intended to get in a jump ahead of them by getting hold of the land first and fast. Doing away with the lengthy business of hiring lawyers to look up and check over deeds and arranging purchasing papers, buying up mortgages and foreclosing on them. For one thing he hadn't the cash to match what the railroad companies would offer a man to part with his land, or the time to conduct lengthy legal negotiations. His was after quick, cash-on-the-barrel-head deals, with the emphasis on not too much cash.

Wilmore Newcombe relied on the use of the big stick. The sell-or-else threat when weasel words failed to convince a home-steader to sell. In Missouri he found plenty of men who would be more than willing to wield the big stick. Men who had been fighting Kansans since '55 and would keep on doing so just for the pleasure it gave them.

TWO

Will Harding saw the wagon lumbering slowly along the trail at the foot of the field he was ploughing. He lifted the reins from his shoulders and growling at the big-footed grey to stay, he walked across the field to meet up with the wagon before the trail cut north to Big Creek and out of the valley.

Will had the dour-faced, flat-eyed look of a man that life hadn't dealt kindly with. Yet his getting less of his fair share of the breaks hadn't broken him or soured his nature. He carried himself stiff-backed, firm stepping as a man half his fifty plus years. Confidently like a man who had fought for the side that had come out on top in the war. Not like a Kansan who had fought for the rebel cause and helped to carry General Albert Sidney Johnson out of the battle line when he had got himself shot attacking the blue bellies' strong point, the Hornets' Nest, at what the Unionists called the Battle of Pittsburgh Landing but what the south knew as the Battle of Shiloh.

He saw the lovable old man die sitting back against a tree calmly watching his life's blood draining away from the wound in his leg. Cried along with the rest of the boys when they buried him. Somehow, though the fighting and the killing was to continue for another three years, Will saw at Shiloh the beginning of the end for his cause, and he braced himself to stick it out, come hell and high water. A man doesn't run out on his buddies when the going gets tough. Hearing about the death of his wife only deepened his inner grimness to take all the shit that was coming his way.

He had come back to the valley a month back, ready to stare down any resentment against him for having fought against the Union.

And that's all he would do. He'd done all

the killing for a cause he could take. To his surprise no one in the valley wanted to tar and feather him, run him out of the territory even though they had lost close kin in the war. They seemed to want to forget about all the bloodshed and sorrow and get back to working their land. Being farmers again, not soldiers. And so they had before trouble hit the valley. Trouble like livestock being killed, barns burnt down and more serious, a man and his boy shot dead on a farm at the southern end of the valley.

To Will the trouble smelt like Missouri raiders work. It was their style. Coming in at night, attacking some isolated homestead, killing and burning out the anti-slavers. Not accepting that the war was over. What puzzled Will was why the raiders had ridden this far into Kansas to do their killing. Their stomping grounds had been the border country. Whoever the raiders were the sons-of-bitches would get a hot reception if they showed up in front of his stoop. Will grimly thought. His two fully loaded Frontier Colt pistols and his big 'fifty' Martin Henry long gun were always within grabbing distance, asleep or awake.

In a slight lifting trail-dust haze the wagon drew up alongside Will. Will touched his hat to the bonnet-wearing elderly woman sitting next to the driver, a bent-shouldered old man with a lined, sun-dried farmer's face. Four youngsters, boys and girls, of various ages, perched among the furniture and crates piled up high in the body of the wagon. Will's face boned over. It wasn't a cheerful, heart warming sight seeing a man leaving the land he'd about broke his back on trying to provide for his family and all he had to show for the long hard years was piled in a heap on the back of a wagon.

'I'm Lucas Bream, neighbour,' the wagon driver said. 'I farmed a good piece to the west of yuhr place. This here is mah good lady wife.' He pointed over his shoulder. 'Back there is mah brood.' He spat a stream of tobacco juice across the rumps of the two-mule team. 'Yuh'll have heard about the shootin' and the burnin'.'

Will nodded. 'I've heard, friend.'

'Well the sonsuvbitches came and hit mah place last night,' Lucas Bream said angrily. 'Kilt Ma's milk cow and all mah hogs. Burnt the house down about us.' The old farmer sent another stream of brown juice arcing across the mules' rears. 'Just managed tuh save what yuh see on the wagon there so ah'm pullin' out. If mah two eldest boys hadn't been kilt in the fightin' at Gettysburg ah might have stayed and took the bastards on. But ah ain't got the balls fur a stand up killin' fight now. Ain't about tuh risk losin' any more of mah family, and that's the truth, neighbour.'

'If you want anything to help you on your way, Mr Bream,' Will said. 'Feed for the mules, rations for you and your family, you're welcome to take some of mine. I ain't got a lot but as I say you're sure welcome to share them.'

'We'll manage, neighbour,' Lucas Bream replied. 'But it's right Christian-minded of

24

yuh to make the offer. Ah've got kin near Wichita so it ain't goin' to be a long haul for us.' He spat again before jerking the reins and setting the wagon rolling once more. His, 'Goodbye, neighbour,' sounding above the rattling of the wagon.

Will walked back to the plough almost wishing that the trouble that had suddenly hit the valley would come his way just to prove to his neighbours that it was trouble for all the valley, ex-rebs as well. He gave a muttered 'damn' and led the grey back to the barn and unhitched the plough. He saddled up the pinto and rein-led it across to the shack, tied it off, then went inside. On coming out he was carrying the big Sharps and one Colt was belted about his middle, the other one stuck down his pants top. He was loaded for bear and intended to do some scouting around the valley. He wasn't about to wait till the marauders came sneaking up to his shack one dark night with flaming torches held in their hands. By going on the offensive, he would, by reading their tracks, get an idea of how many men were involved in the raiding, the trails they used to get into the valley. He had done many a suchlike scout during the war behind the Union lines. Knowing what he was up against gave him a chance either to make a fight of it or, if the odds were too great, pull out like Lucas Bream. Though, he grimly thought, they'd need a whole company of the sons-of-bitches to make him pull up stakes and quit his land and leave his wife's grave on the hill at the back of the shack to grow wild and forgotten.

THREE

Ira gave out a loud groan of relief. He was nearing the end of his ball-aching journey, back on his land once more. To his right he saw a shack, a thin trace of smoke coming from its stack, and freshly worked land. Will Harding's place. Leastways it was before the war. He slow-grinned. The awkward old cuss had sure caused a stir in the valley by going off to fight for Jeff Davis and the newly formed Confederated States of America.

Ira remembered him as a solid block of a man. Glum-faced as though always expecting the worst out of life. He had been one of the first homesteaders in the valley. Fought Indians to hold on to his land. Activities not calculated to bring a smile to any man's face. Then life had dealt Will the bitterest blow of

27

all. Four years of putting his life on the line for a cause that was lost and gone.

He hoped it was Will back there in the shack. He bore him no emnity for they had been confusing, heady days. A man had to make his own decisions, pay no heed to sometimes his close kin's views let alone neighbours'. Do what he felt right as he saw it. Though as the war lengthened, became even bloodier, he'd had doubts about his and Will's strongly held views being worth all the maiming and killing. Right now he didn't give a damn if Jeff Davis and old General Robert E Lee were ploughing the next field to his.

When he got settled in his place he would ride over and pay Will a visit. Not that they'd been real close neighbours though Will and his wife had come and paid their respects at his ma and pa's funeral and had offered to join the posse that had been raised to hunt down the band of Cheyenne broncos that had jumped their buggy on the trail from Plainsville but just to show them that as far as he was concerned the war had never been.

Closing in on his shack Ira drew up his mount and gave the land he had not seen for nigh on four years a long, welcoming look. His fields, as he'd expected, had grown wild, lengths of fencing were down, planks missing in the feed barn's sides. As far as he could see from this distance the shack didn't seem in too bad a shape. It could still be lived in. To his surprise there were three horses in the corral and like Will Harding's place smoke was coming out of the stack.

Ira wondered how that could be. None of his neighbours knew that he was coming home, didn't even know that he'd survived the war. Unless someone was seeing to it that the shack didn't become derelict.

He didn't recognize the three men that stepped on to the porch at his approach as valley folk he'd known before the war. M'be, he thought, they were newcomers. Closer to them that thought was quickly dispelled. The trio were shut-faced, unshaven-visaged men wearing heavy pistols in well filled shell belts about their middles that pulled at their pants tops. Whoever they were, Ira was sure they didn't earn their keep by raising hogs or walking behind a plough.

Silently they fish-eyed him as he pulled up his horse, though remaining mounted, several yards short of the shack. Then he began to get angry. He hadn't come through the war just to let three hard-faced saddle-tramps squat on his property. 'This happens to be my land you're making yourselves at home on! And I've got papers to prove it!' he snapped out.

The three men looked at each other then grinned as though they had just been told a ribald joke.

'Mister,' the man on Ira's extreme left said. 'Possession is ten tenths of the law, the way we see it. Me and my buddies came across this abandoned shack and we just naturally moved in.' He glanced along at his two buddies, a look that set them all grinning widely again. 'If you mean those papers in the tin box behind that loose brick in the chimney stack, pilgrim,' he continued, 'well they kinda got burnt up being me and the boys reckoned that the asshole who owned this rattrap musta got himself killed in the war.' The grins slowly switched off. When the man spoke again his voice was hard and menacing. 'You ain't thinkin' of pushing your luck and disputing our rights of ownership, mister?' His hand dropped threateningly on to the butt of his pistol.

Even if he'd been a fast draw man Ira knew that it was too late for him to make a fight for it. A flapped cavalry holster wasn't made for a quick draw. And he hadn't a snowball's chance in hell of yanking out his rifle before the three ugly-faced bastards used him for target practice. Whether he liked it or not, and the war proved he had grit, Ira knew that it was crow-eating time.

Through his glasses Will Harding took in the scene at the front of the shack. Earlier he had picked up the signs of at least nine, ten riders on one of the back trails into the valley. Tracks, he opined, of men who didn't want their presence in the valley known. The riders had split up, he followed the smaller bunch, and now it seemed that he had caught up with the back-trail riding bastards. That they'd come into the valley to do harm was clear the way the three of them were crowding Ira Brooks. Like him, it seemed that he'd come back from the war all in one piece and it wasn't right at all that the kid should be shot down like a dog in front of his own shack. He'd worked hard to make a go of the farm when his pa and ma were killed by Indians. Will dropped back off the ridge, mounted up, and rode in a wide arc to come up on the shack face on.

Suppressing his rage or he would do something foolish that would get him killed, Ira gave the three mock-smiling raiders a drop-dead glare and turned his mount's head round to ride away. To go some place where he could think out some plan for getting hold of his shack and land again and stay alive long enough to work on it.

A resounding boom from the rim of the dry wash that cut across his land to his rear stayed his hand. The man who had been doing the talking was flung back against the shack wall as though buffeted by a blast from a twister. Rebounding back with arms outstretched to fall off the porch and land with a dirt-raising thud on the ground, back ripped open, bloodied and dead. By then Ira was out of the saddle hunkered down behind the water trough, pistol fisted and firing, backing up his hidden ally.

The two men left on the porch got over their initial shock at the sudden change of events and crouching low, they cut loose with their pistols. The hidden big gun boomed again and another of the raiders felt the smashing, chest caving, impact of Will's Sharps' heavy lead slug.

The last man decided to make a real fight of it. Mouthing obscenities he jumped off the porch and ran at Ira, firing wildly as he came. Calmly Ira laid his pistol across his left forearm, drew a bead on him, and triggered off a single shot. The charging man faltered in his stride as a spasm of infinite agony screwed up his face into a gargoyle-like mask, cutting short his half-voiced yell of pain. Somehow, with his pistol hanging limply by his side, he managed four tangle-footed steps forward as the red stain spread rapidly across his shirt front. As he stumbled on he slowly sank to his knees and pitched forward on to his face, his body ceasing all movement.

Will Harding climbed out of the wash and Ira saw who his ally was. With his Sharps held at the high port Will walked across to Ira, keeping a watchful eye on the three crumpled-up bodies. He cold-smiled Ira.

'Welcome home, neighbour,' he said.

Ira gave him an equally tight-faced smile back. 'Ain't quite the homecoming I expected, Mr Harding,' he said. 'Like you, I reckon, I've had more than a belly-full of getting shot at. Who are they? Missouri brush boys still carrying the big hate for us Kansas anti-slavers?'

'Could be, Mr Brooks,' Will replied. 'Can't see Kansas men killing and burning out their own kind.' He then told Ira about the shooting down of the homesteader and his son and the reasons for Lucas Bream quitting his land.

When Ira mentioned that the three dead men had been claiming squatters' rights on his land Will's face boned over in anger. 'It seems more than the settling up of old scores. It looks as though some sonuvabitch is tryin' his hand at landgrabbing. What for I don't rightly know. There's plenty of grass outside the valley for ranchers to feed their beef on without resorting to bloodshed to get hold of what there is here, Mr Brooks. Whoever it is and whatever he wants the valley for it must be something real big. Those hombres we've just shot don't come cheap.'

'What do we do with them, Mr Harding?' Ira said.

'I ain't about to raise any sweat-breaking ground giving them a regular buryin',' Will replied. 'We'll tarp-wrap them and sling them across their mounts. I reckon the horses will find their way back to where they were last fed.' He gave a mirthless toothy grin. 'I opine that the sight of their dead compadres will show the rest of the bully boys that they ain't about to get it all their own way.' Will shrugged his shoulders. 'Whether that will put an end to their raidin' I don't rightly know. We can only wait and see, and keep our powder dry.'

FOUR

Jake Mills rubbed a tongue-licked finger over the foresight of the Spencer. He reached up slightly, keeping his head to one side of the open window, and laid the rifle on the ledge. Left eye shut, right eye squinting along the barrel at the bunch of riders silhouetted like stone-chiselled figures on the ridge above his shack, he triggered off the full seven loads the Spencer held.

Cursing loudly Phil Clinton dropped low across his saddle as a slug hissed dangerously close to his head. Tex Hobbs, the rider alongside him gave out a howl of pain and rocked in his saddle clutching at his right shoulder.

'Get the hell off this ridge, boys!' Clinton yelled. 'Before that sonuvabitch blasts us off it!'

His boys didn't need any urging. The hail of Spencer shells whizzing about their ears, nicking horses' flanks, setting them kicking and squealing with pain, almost unseating their riders, cleared them from the skyline as though swept off by a charge of grapeshot. Clinton angrily thought that more sneaky tactics would be needed to get the sharpshooting bastard off his piece of land. Wilmore Newcombe, sitting on his big fat ass back in Missouri, would have to put his timetable back somewhat.

Phil Clinton was a small, thin-shouldered, snake-eyed man. Making up for his physical smallness in his largeness in mental vicious meanness. He had been killing the Kansas nigger-lovers for the past eight years. Did it for the pleasure it gave him. Getting paid to do it was the cherry on the cake. But that didn't mean that he still hadn't to look out for number one. He wasn't about to try and clear the valley of the Yankee sodbusters like some liquored-up bronco. Mad-assed actions like that could get him killed.

Till now the operation had been going smoothly. One sodbuster and his brood pulling out of the valley, the other family whose menfolk were killed by him he reckoned would soon get the message that farming in Big Creek valley was an occupation that held no future for them, not enjoyable ones anyway. And Skip and two of the boys were occupying the abandoned shack. Then that bastard in the shack below the ridge had to go and cut loose at them, showing that some of the sodbusters were ready for them and prepared to push it to a fight.

That the sodbusters couldn't be caught napping worried Clinton for a while then he gave a cold, lip-curling grin. What the hell did he expect? A walkover? He was still fighting the bloody war and his raiding was bound to invite trouble from men who like him were prepared to keep the war going.

Then again it was still a lot easier than it was in those days. Then they had to dodge blue belly patrols to get back into Missouri to hole up in some draughty backwoods barn. Now the boys after a raid could ride high, wide and handsome, into Plainsville and whoop it up there and buy drinks for off-duty blue belly soldier boys and Kansas cattlemen.

'OK, boys,' he said. 'Let's head back to Plainsville and get your busted shoulder seen to, Tex. We'll come back when it's real dark like and give that sodbuster and his family down there a taste of Missouri brush boy hurrahin'.'

Jake kept an alert eye on the ridge, the Spencer reloaded, ready to send another full load screeching up at the riders if they so much as poked their horses' noses over the rimline.

'Any signs of the jayhawkers from your side, Ben?' Jake called, without taking his gaze from his sighting. Like Ira and Will, Jake had opined that the men that were killing and burning in the valley could only be Missouri irregulars. Men that ten years of killing hadn't quenched their hatred.

Ben, Jake's only boy (Jake had lost three older boys fighting for the Union) stuck his head out of the back window of the shack for a quick look up the hillside. 'No, Pa,' he said and drew his head back in again.

Jake gave a noncommittal grunt. 'They was allus dirty night-riding sonsuvbitches. Ain't got the balls to face a man in daylight. Liked to do their dirty work on some dark back trail. But keep a watchful eye out, they might be getting overconfident and starting to do their raiding in daylight.'

Being alert, day and night, had been an integral part of Jake Mills' life. He had come to eastern Kansas in the late fifties when not to be alert was asking to be butchered by a Cheyenne warband. Before that he had farmed on land near the Missouri border. His farm being a way station on the underground railroad for liberated Negro slaves from the south. Those days a man had to sleep standing up, one eye open, a fully loaded Beecher's bible, a Sharps rifle, near

41

at hand, if he didn't want his shack burnt down and him and his male kin strung up by the neck in his own orchard by Missouri raiders.

Jake had heard of the killings in the valley that had forced Lucas Bream to quit his land, so he made sure he was good and ready for what trouble might come his way before it really got serious. Like throwing down on the bunch of riders on the ridge. Valley folk didn't ride about in bunches and didn't skulk along back-trail ridges. He was willing to kiss ass later if they turned out to be genuine drifters or cattlemen. Eating humble pie was a long way better than being dead.

Faintly, on the light breeze blowing from the south, Ira heard the snare drum-like raps of a single fast shooting rifle. The horses had been rump-slapped off, carrying their macabre loads, and Ira was about to have his first look inside his home since leaving for the war. He stopped dead in his stride, hand on the door latch. 'Hear that, Mr Harding?' he said.

'I hear,' Will said grimly. 'Sounds like it's comin' from old Jake Mills' place. M'be he could need some help. There's only him and a young boy to defend his holding.'

'As I said, Mr Harding,' Ira said. 'It ain't what I expected, getting shot at and having to start killin' men all over again, when I came home. But if that's the way things are turning out I ain't about to sit on my ass and let whoever it is that's causing trouble call all the shots. I reckon we should ride over and give Mr Mills a helping hand. He was an old friend of my pa.' Ira gave a lopsided grin. 'I ain't seen the inside of my home for a long time, Mr Harding, putting off that pleasure for a while longer won't hurt me none. That's if you don't mind leaving your wife again.'

'My wife died a while back, Mr Brooks,' Will said. 'I've got all the time in the world.' And he swung up on to his horse.

Before Ira could say that he was sorry to

hear of Mrs Harding's death Will was riding away.

Jake, with Ben standing alongside him on the porch, rifles held loosely across their chests, grinned up at Ira and Will. 'I rightly appreciate you ridin' across to give us a hand, neighbours, but the trouble's over.' Jake pointed over his shoulder. 'A while back I spotted a bunch of riders up on that ridge. I smelt that they were trouble so I didn't let them get in any closer. I just cut loose at the sonsuvbitches with the Spencer. Ain't seen hide nor hair of them since.'

'Mr Brooks has had some trouble with what could be part of the same bunch you scared away, Jake,' Will said. He then told him of the killing of the three men occupying Ira's shack.

'Well I'll be...' exclaimed Jake. 'It smells like landgrabbin'.'

'That's what me and Mr Brooks reckons,' Will said.

Jake narrow-eyed Ira. 'The asshole in

44

charge won't like his boys being killed, Mr Brooks. It kinda knocks the shine off the operation, no matter how high the pay is. They can't spend it wrapped up in a blanket lyin' in Boot Hill. They'll come back fast to stomp on you real hard to frighten off any other homesteader that's thinkin' about making a fight of it. And to get blood for blood to make things even.

'I wouldn't dispute that reasoning, Mr Mills,' Ira replied. 'But I'll be more than ready for them next time round.' Cold-smiling he continued, 'We took enough guns off those fellas we shot to arm the garrison of a small fort.'

Will's face creased in doubt. 'M'be the pair of you are right but you, Jake, won't be far down on the gang's list for getting even with either. We've got to outthink the sonsuvbitches. Try and figure out who they'll hit next and be there when they do it to help out. There's not enough of us to watch out for the whole valley.'

Jake gazed at Will for a while before

answering him. Then he gave up trying to understand the workings of some fellas' minds. Will Harding not so long back was doing his damnedest to kill the kin of the homesteaders in the valley, now he was prepared to put his life on the line to protect them. 'You've got a point there, Mr Harding,' he said. 'If they're landgrabbers the next piece of land I reckon on their list, not counting the upset you and the kid's given them, will be the widow McDowell's place. She's there with only her daughter and two young boys, not as old as Ben here. The murderin' bastards shot her man and her oldest boy. She's got no chance, no chance at all if they jump her. But I still favour them visiting Ira first, and soon.'

Will's face tightened with resolve as he reached his decision. 'I think I'll ride across to the widow's place,' he said. 'That's if she don't mind an ex-Johnny Reb helping her out. Could surprise the sonsuvbitches when they find themselves not just up against a woman and three kids. M'be scare them off

46

so we can win some time to get the folk in the valley organized and take them on our own terms.' Will turned to Ira. 'That's if you'll be OK on your own, Mr Brooks?'

Ira grinned. 'All you rebs couldn't stop me from coming back to my land. A few sneaky assholes who liked to call themselves Confederate soldiers have no chance at all in chasing me off my property. You go and help the widow lady, Mr Harding. How about you, Mr Mills? You must have got their dander up by firing on them. They could come fireballing down on you next.'

Jake spat dispassionately in the dirt at his feet. 'Just let the sidewinders come. There's Ben and me, and ma. Ma was right annoyed when she couldn't take a hand in the shootin'. She can handle a long gun real purty. Had to. When me and Mr Harding first came to the valley there was a lot of Injun trouble goin' on. Grandpappys, grandmas, youngsters over ten year old were standin' at the loopholes or loading guns.'

'OK, Jake, that's settled then,' Will said.

'We'll check out what you need in the way of firearms, Mr Brooks, and I'll take what you don't want. I'll go and see to my stock and pick up my warbag and bedroll before I head for the widow's place.'

FIVE

Will approached the McDowell homestead while it was still light – not wishing to scare the widow by showing up out of the dark, or alarm her sufficiently to pull off a shot at him. Another thought was souring his face. He'd had no trouble from any of the homesteaders since returning home, but that didn't mean everyone in the valley had forgiven him for fighting for the South. Mrs McDowell could class him no better than the white trash who had gunned down her husband and son. He couldn't rightly blame her. The way she saw it they were ex-Johnny Rebs just like he was.

He halted his horse and called, 'Hullo the house! It's me, Will Harding. My holding's next to Jake Mills, beside the crick. I've ridden over to see if you want any help. You might have heard that I was a reb. But for me the war's over, and that's the honest truth, ma'am.'

Slowly the shack door creaked open and Mrs McDowell stepped into view holding a rifle in her hand. Meg had faced danger and death before, on the wagon train coming to the valley, fighting off bad Indians. Though then she'd had a man to give her strength. On her own, with her daughter and two young boys to protect, she was shaken by real fear. Now a man she vaguely knew as a farmer at the north of the valley, openly admitting that he'd fought for the South, a fact she was well aware of, was offering to help her.

Meg gave the squat, sombre-faced rider a long weighing-up look. She saw nothing in his make-up that increased her fears. Just the opposite. Mr Harding's quiet, matter-of-fact appearance somehow eased them slightly.

'You step down, Mr Harding,' she said. 'Beth!' she called over her shoulder. 'Set another place at the table, we have a welcome guest. You boys see to Mr Harding's horse.'

Will give her a wide-faced smile as he dismounted and Meg McDowell thought that she was seeing another man.

Ira set about preparing his defences after Will had left, taking with him one of the extra rifles and two of the pistols. Ira wasn't too foolhardy not to realize the deadly risk he was taking if the raiders came but as Will Harding had stated it was kind of a war they were fighting and in a war the risks came up with the rations. As a good soldier he would have to think of tactics that would give him all the edge one man would need against a bunch of men intending to do him harm.

In his favour he had plenty of guns and ammunition and knew the lie of the land around his shack. He had no intention of sitting on his ass inside it and fight them from there. The shack was no strongpoint. They'd burn him out in no time at all. Leaving him only the choice of how he wanted to die, burnt alive, or cut down by lead if he came out into the open. Outside the shack, with the advantage of mobility, essential in all military operations, big or small, he had the extra edge that if they hit him at night in the dark every man he heard he could shoot at. The raiders would be hindered by knowing if they fired at moving shadows they could be hitting each other.

Ira chose the dry wash, the section that snaked round the south end of the shack to make his stand. From there he could cover two sides of the shack. There he placed a rifle and a pistol. He moved higher up the wash till he had a clear sighting of the rear of his shack. Reckoning that it would be the ideal spot for another firing position he made it his second arms cache. He could now lay fire down on three sides of his shack. Stepping out of the wash Ira began gathering up armfuls of dead brushwood and laid it out in a line several yards in front of the shack. Searching in his barns he found several cans of coal oil, each containing a drain of oil, enough to give the brushwood a good dousing. He studied the ground for a while figuring out how the raiders would come at him. Above the shack was a stand of timber, good cover if the moon was high and clear, for a bunch of riders to get real close to the shack. Ira took his rope from his saddle and strode up to the trees. He tight-stretched the rope, horse-knee high, across the trail just before it came out into the open. One end of the rope he fastened to the trigger of a cocked rifle jammed in the fork of a tree. Ira grinned. If he got real lucky m'be he would get one of the raiders. In any case its firing would warn him of approaching danger so giving him a chance of snatching a few hours' sleep during his night-long vigil.

Coming down from the trees Ira stepped on to his porch and surveyed his firing positions with an expertise that he had developed over the war years, an acumen that had kept him alive. He reckoned he was as ready as he could ever be, exploiting every advantage open to him. It was praying time now for all the luck coming his way he could get. Then he went inside his shack for the first time since he left it to enlist in the Union army.

Dirty plates, pots, half-eaten food, and empty bean cans littered the kitchen table. Both bedrooms had been used, the blankets on the unmade beds flung back. Saddle gear and soiled clothes were strewn across the living room floor. The men he and Will Harding had shot must have lived here for some time. It was a far cry from the clean, tidy, fresh-smelling shack his ma had kept. The dirty sons-of-bitches deserved to be shot.

Darkness was dropping in fast, time for him to begin his night watch. He made himself a large pot of coffee, cleaned a cup, took a storm lantern from a nail on the wall, then picked up a blanket from one of the beds. He took a last look round the room as if trying to regain some of the memories it held for him. His face hardened in controlled anger. No Missouri renegades would take it from him as long as he could aim and fire a gun.

Ira dropped down into the wash at his first firing position and lay back against the bank and slowly drank his coffee. His blood was running high, hoping that the raiders would show up and put an end to the trouble he'd unwittingly got himself into, one way or the other. He wrapped the blanket around him and like the veteran blue belly he had once been soon fell into a light sleep.

Ira jerked awake. It was full light. He remembered seeing the hint of dawn in the night sky then he must have fallen asleep when he should have been wide awake. No more, he reckoned, than twenty or thirty minutes or so but full scale battles had been won and lost in far less time. He cursed himself for his lack of alertness. Cautiously he peered over the rim of the wash. The shack was as he had last seen it, still looking deserted. Though that didn't mean there were no men hiding behind the barns waiting for whoever they thought was inside the shack to step out on to the porch. As far as the marauders knew, if they'd caught up with the horses carrying their dead buddies, the shack could be full of armed home-steaders all set to blast away at any strangers coming within rifle range so it would pay them to lie low till they knew for sure what they were facing.

Pinched-assed nerved Ira waited, motion-less, watching for any signs of belly-crawling men among the outbuildings. In the dark the wash had been an ideal firing position; come daylight it was a deathtrap, easily enfiladed by gunfire from either end. Finally convinced that no danger was close by, no one who could draw a bead on him when he showed himself, Ira picked up the extra weapons, leaving the lantern, and clambered out of the wash and walked back to the shack.

Inside the shack he placed a rifle and pistol at the rear window and did likewise at the only side window. After a quickly prepared and eaten meal, of beans and coffee, he came out and sat down on the edge of the front porch, rifle resting across his knees and finished drinking his coffee. Black and strong to keep himself awake. All the while hawk-eyeing the trail that led out of the tree. The hogpen state of his home would have to wait. Staying alive came before cleanliness. He'd discovered that the hard way during the war.

The two riders closing in on the shack at a steady canter brought Ira to his feet with his rifle swinging up into a firing position. He lowered it again when he recognized one of the riders as Jake's son, Ben. His companion, a boy not much older than Ben, was a newcomer to him.

'Howdye, Mr Brooks,' Ben said, as they drew up alongside the porch. 'Pa sent me and Pat Levins, his pa runs the next farm to ours, across to keep a watch out for you while you have some shuteye. But first we're goin' on to Mr Harding's place to feed and water his stock. He's stayin' at the widow McDowell's another night.'

'Did the raiders pay you or the widow a visit last night, Ben?' Ira asked.

'Naw,' Ben replied. 'And pa said, when he came back from the McDowells' place, he let Mr Harding know that we'd see to his stock, they'd be no trouble either. How about you, Mr Brooks? Did they bother you?'

'No they didn't, Ben,' Ira said. Sensing both boys' eagerness to get the chance to throw-down on the raiders he thanked God that the war was over or the pair of them could have ended up all torn and bloodied, dead, in front of some reb entrenchment.

'I'm real obliged to your pa, Ben, and both of you,' he said. 'I sure ain't as young as I was and I could do with some sleep or I won't last another night's watch out. But two hours, no more, understand? And if you see riders' dust angling this way you wake me, pronto.' Ira hard-eyed the two boys. 'It ain't some game we're playin'. We could get ourselves dead.'

'We'll wake you, Mr Brooks,' Ben said.

'And don't worry about us keepin' a good lookout. Pat will go up on the ridge. From there he can spot a jack-rabbit movin' around.'

'Good,' said Ira. 'I'll look out for you coming back.' Ira gave them another warning. 'But if you hear any gunfire don't come barging in. As I said this is for real. We're pitting ourselves up against some genuine mean stompin' men. Grandma throat-slitters to a man. So you just haul-ass back to your pa's place and tell him to get forted up.'

'We'll do that, Mr Brooks.' Ben gazed with smooth-faced innocence at Ira then exchanged glances with Pat. 'Ain't that so, Pat?'

'Sure thing, Ben,' Pat said equally open-faced.

You young bastards, thought Ira, you've no intention of doing what I've told you. The pair of you are lying through your back teeth. He knew it was a waste of time to press his orders any stronger. Looking at the boys he was seeing himself as he used to be. Stubborn-minded as a Missouri mule. At least he'd warned them.

'Oh, I nearly forgot, Mr Brooks,' said Ben. 'I had to give you these.' He handed down to Ira a small tar-paper wrapped parcel. 'Two sticks of blasting powder, left over after we'd cleared one of our fields of tree stumps.' Ben grinned. 'Pa said they should still be able to make a big bang.'

Ira handled the parcel gingerly. 'As long as it don't make that big bang in my hand,' he said sourly.

Ben, still smiling, said, 'Come on Pat, let's ride and get our chores done then we can get back here and let this old man have his sleep.'

'Why you young...' Ira said, then started grinning himself.

Will, after spending the night on an alert but undisturbed vigil in a small shed facing the house, was now sleeping between clean white sheets in a proper bed in Mrs

McDowell's back bedroom after another meal the widow had made for him. It was only the second time Will had sat down and eaten off a linen-laid table and a meal prepared by a woman since his wife had died.

When Mrs McDowell had invited him to dismount and come indoors Will had put it to her that although he'd come to help her he was only one man. If the marauders did come, through the off-putting surprise his extra firepower would have on them, they expecting only token resistance, or none, from a widow woman, he could m'be hold them off for one attack. But they'd be back he told her, so it was in his considered opinion it would save her and her kids a whole heap of grief if she packed up her belongings and moved in with one of the other families in the valley till the trouble was over. Or leave the valley for good. The widow McDowell's eyes had flared up in anger at his suggestion.

'M'be you're right, Mr Harding,' she said

firmly. 'But I'm not leaving my home. Those scum murdered my man and eldest boy. They died for this piece of land and I'm not about to waste their dying. We'll stay here till they burn us out. I'm truly thankful for your offer of help but I don't want you thinking that you're about to risk your own life because a poor widow woman is too pride–stubborn to see sense.'

For some inexplicable reason Will began to compare Meg McDowell with his late wife, Jane. They both had the same fight-back temperament, the same strong, careworn features of a real true grit plainswoman that still held some of their former youthful beauty.

'You ain't stubborn at all in wanting to hold on to your land, ma'am,' Will said. 'But you more than anyone in the valley know what that could mean for you. If you're willin' to take that risk then I'm willin' to make a stand with you. It's not just your fight, it's the whole valley's fight. It just happens that the next battle could be fought right here.'

'I had to know how you felt, Mr Harding,' Mrs McDowell said. 'I thought that because you'd fought for the South you felt that you owed us valley folk...' Her voice trailed away.

Will slowly shook his head. 'No, ma'am. I ain't makin' amends for my sinful ways. It's as I said. It's the Big Creek's fight and if we stick together we can beat the sonsuv ... beggin' your pardon, ma'am, the raiders.'

'I'm glad,' Mrs McDowell said. 'I wouldn't have wanted your help any other way. The war is over for me too.'

A slight smile lightened up Will's dour features. 'Someone else told me the same thing earlier on in the day. M'be before the night's out we'll get that message to the fellas that's doin' the killin' and the burnin'.'

Mrs McDowell's smile was warmer. 'Just one thing, Mr Harding, I'm Mrs McDowell or Meg, not ma'am. Ma'am makes me feel like an old schoolmarm.'

Will hesitated before answering then

surprised at his boldness he said. 'Meg it is then, if it's Will to you. Now we'll get down to discussing the business that brought me here.' Will's face had slipped back into its normal grim lines. 'I intend to make my stand in the barn out front, Meg. I've brought extra guns but they're mainly to make a lot of noise with. I don't want you and the kids to show yourselves more than it's necessary to poke a gun through a window and blaze away at thin air. I'll do all the real shootin' that's required.'

Meg found herself thinking along the same lines Will had been doing. Comparing him, practically a stranger, with her husband. All she knew about him was that he'd fought for the rebs and was a widower. He'd the same basic qualities, solid, dependable, a rock to lean on in bad times. Meg gave an involuntary shudder. Qualities that had got her husband an early grave, and could get Mr Will Harding likewise. Meg kept those frightening thoughts from showing in her face.

'I understand, Will,' she said. 'We'll do as you say. Now we've talked enough, let's go and eat, Beth will have the meal ready by now.'

Will waited till full light before he came out of the barn and not before he had given the homestead surroundings a long searching look. It had been an uneventful watch but it didn't do to take chances against sneaky operators like ex-Missouri bush boys. They could have come in close during the night and were now biding their time before attacking the shack. Satisfied that there was no danger to Meg and her family Will stepped out of the barn and walked across to the house, greeted by an appetising smell of frying bacon and beans and freshly brewed coffee.

'I take it that you'll be wanting to go and see to your own chores, Will,' Meg said while they were eating. 'We'll be all right now, in the daytime.' Meg gave a wan smile. 'Though I admit that I was so scared last night I hardly slept. And worried that coming here could get you killed.' Meg's face coloured up like a bashful young girl's and she hurried away from the table and almost ran into the kitchen.

'Well I'll be...,' Will said. He'd come to protect a shack from being burnt down. Now he felt that he was protecting a family as though he was the man of the house. Which gave him a good, proud feeling, a feeling of belonging. Emotions that hadn't come his way for a long time.

Jake Mills showing up and telling him that his boy was willing to go to his place and see to the stock gave Will the excuse, no longer unexplainable, to spend the rest of the day with Meg. When he had told Jake that it had been a quiet night he asked if Ira had been attacked.

'Not that I heard, Mr Harding,' Jake said. 'But my boy will pay him a call to find out for sure on the ride to your holding. Ask him if he wants him to stand watch while he gets some sleep.'

After accepting a cup of coffee, Jake, wishing Will good shooting if the gang put in an appearance, bade him and Meg a 'goodbye' and rode back to his holding.

'There's no need for you to stay all day, Will, or tonight for that matter.' Meg white-lied. 'It could be your place they attack next.'

Will didn't tell her that he had powerful feelings telling him otherwise. He used to get them during the war, especially during the Wilderness campaign along the Orange Plank road. Everything would be all peaceful, birds singing their hearts out, butterflies hovering on every bush, yet still he couldn't fully unwind. Then before a man could spit, Grant's blue belly rough-riding horse soldiers would come fire-balling out of the woods and the killing would start up again.

'If they hit my place there's only an old shack to burn down. Here they can destroy a family and that as sure as hell can't be rebuilt.'

For the second time Meg had to make a

dash for the kitchen to hide her emotions. After a while she came back into the living-room, eyes red with weeping, carrying a blanket.

'You can sleep in the spare room, Will,' she said. 'There's sheets on it but you'll need this blanket. The boys can keep watch till you've rested.'

'There ain't no need to put yourself out, Meg,' protested Will. 'I'll make do in the barn. I've slept in less comfortable places.'

'You're a welcome guest in my house, Will Harding,' Meg said firmly. 'And guests don't sleep in barns. Leastways the McDowell family guests don't,' she added, smiling.

SIX

The Phil Clinton gang were bellied up against the Plainsville Saloon bar, the setback at the valley still rankling Phil. The half bottle of Old Crow he had downed only aggravated his guts still further. Tex's shoulder wound had been treated and the doc had warned him that he had to keep off his horse for a week or so or the wound would open up again. That still left the gang eleven strong, counting Skip and the two boys with him in the abandoned shack. He'd ride back to the valley as soon as it got dark, pick up the boys in the shack, then hit the sharp-shooting sodbuster real good and hard.

Eleven men should be enough to do that. With his meanness working at full blast Phil intended to make a night of it by clearing the widow woman and her kids off her land. Skip and Bilby's chore. He was taking another pull at the whisky when Tex burst into the saloon and hurried over to the bar to tell that Skip, Bilby and Swaine had returned to Plainsville strapped across their horses well and truly plugged.

Phil's face screwed up tight as though in pain and he cursed long and hard, and changed his war plans. 'Drink up, boys,' he snarled. 'Meet me out front in ten minutes.' He gave the line of drinkers a snake-eyed look. 'Armed up real good. We've got a heavy night comin' up. See to my horse, Tex, I've some business to see to.'

The business Phil was seeing to was the hiring of two extra men. Hired hands that would see to it that the widow vacated her holding. He wanted all his boys with him. He'd finished pussyfooting around with the sodbusters in the valley. The first sodbuster to feel the full weight of his 'black flag' boys would be the son-of-bitch that had gunned down Skip and his two buddies. Then they'd move on to the holding where they'd been fired upon. Stomp him out for ever before going through the valley like the blue belly bastard general, Sherman, stormed through Georgia, leaving it all smoking and burning.

It was still daylight when Will walked across to the barn to take up his night post. When Meg had woken him, after letting him sleep longer than he'd told her to, he felt surprisingly refreshed – considering he'd gone to bed worrying in case he'd bitten off more than he could chew in defending the McDowell homestead. Giving Meg the false hope that she and her family would come to no harm.

'There's a meal ready, Will,' Meg said.

Will smiled. 'I swear I've never eaten so well since our outfit captured a blue belly supply wagon outside Chattanooga near the end of the war. But right now a cup of coffee will do me fine. Being hungry keeps a man awake.'

Before leaving the shack Will saw to it that

all the guns were checked out and again told Meg to make sure that she and the children stayed low if the marauders came.

Buzz and Elliot, the two men that Phil had hired, weren't really genuine hardcases. They made a living by lifting the occasional longhorn or two, rolling drunks in dark alleys. Mean stomping men if the odds were two to one in their favour. Chasing a woman and her kids out of their home, Buzz opined, didn't warrant scrabbling about in the dark like a couple of bare-assed broncos on a hair-lifting raid.

'We ride right up to the widow's front porch, Elliot,' he said. 'Give her ten minutes to get what she wants out of the shack on to a wagon then we put a torch to the place. Should be back in Plainsville spending our due in no time at all.' Buzz thought of a particular whore who would treat him real special when he flashed the dollar bills around.

Elliot only grunted in reply. He was

thinking that if he got real mean and threatening, the widow might be persuaded to show him some extra special favours just so that he wouldn't hurt her kids none. Elliot didn't believe in paying out hard cash for pleasures that could be had for free if the right pressure was applied.

Will saw the twin dust-trails coming up the track to the farm. He took a hurried look round but saw no signs of any more horsemen. He shouted a warning to Meg. 'There's two riders comin' in! Could be homesteaders paying you a visit to see if you're OK. But keep your heads down unless you know them as neighbours. If they're not yell at them to get off your land. Then I'll take over from then on, understand?'

Buzz cursed out loud when he saw two rifles and two pistols poking out of the windows of the shack pointing at him and Elliot. That weasel-faced son-of-a-bitch, Phil Clinton, said it would be a walkover, no men in the shack. From where he was sitting it didn't look that way. He pulled up his horse, Elliot moving a little to one side of him before he too drew his mount to a halt.

Meg cast a quick glance at her children, her confident smile only showing as a stiff-faced nervous grin. 'Don't worry,' she whispered, 'Mr Harding will see that we come to no harm.' Raising her voice she called out, 'Get off my land, or my men will fire on you!'

Buzz hungfire on his cursing, giving an oily smile instead. 'We're just a coupla out of work ranch-hands passing through. Just want to water our horses, that's all. Ain't no need to get all-fired tetchy, ma'am.'

'You heard the lady,' Will said. 'Ride out while you still can, friends.'

Buzz and Elliot swivelled-ass in their saddles to see a square-built man step out of the barn holding a pistol on them. Buzz resumed his cursing of Phil Clinton. It sure didn't look like it was going to be easy money.

'Now there ain't no need to pull a pistol

on us, mister,' Buzz said. 'As I told the lady we only want her say-so for us to set down and water our horses.' He took a chance at another smile. His face muscles loosened into something that resembled a friendly grin while his right hand sneaked down to the pistol sheathed on his right hip.

Will fired and Buzz died, completely out of character for a man of his ilk, with a smile on his face. Elliot's hands grabbed at air as Buzz fell out of his saddle. White-faced he mouthed hoarsely, 'I ain't about to go for my gun, mister, honest I ain't.'

Will kept the pistol fixed on him. Fish-eyeing Elliot he growled, 'Any more of you scum hangin' round here?'

'No, just me and Buzz,' Elliot replied. 'We was told that there'd only be a widow woman and her kids here and the two of us would have no trouble shiftin' her off her land.' The hard look he was getting was unnerving Elliot. It was kiss-ass time. 'We weren't goin' to hurt the lady, mister. In fact me and Buzz were goin' to help her put her bits and pieces on the wagon, hitch up the mules for her. We was told to treat her real gentle like.'

'I'll just bet that you won't be goin' to hurt her,' Will said sarcastically. 'Like your buddy, Buzz, there in the dirt, had no intention of doing me harm. Who's payin' you to do this lowdown skunk's work?'

'A mean-faced bastard called Phil Clinton,' Elliot said. 'Has about eight or so Missourian hard-cases riding with him, though one of them is in Plainsville nursing a bullet wound in his shoulder. He'd three more boys but someone shot them all dead and wrapped them up neat and tidy like on their horses and sent them into town. That's why me and Buzz got hired.' Elliot's blood chilled over. A gut-feeling was telling him that he was being eyeballed by one of the 'someones' that had done the shooting. But he'd be damned if he was going to tell the Indian-faced bastard about his suspicions in case it upset him and he started to use the big Colt he was fisting on him. 'The gang

76

hangs out in the Plainsville saloon when they're in town. And that's all I know about them, mister,' Elliot finished off.

'Do you know what mischief this fella Clinton and his wild boys are brewing up for us valley folk right now?' Will asked.

'I've told you all I know, mister, and that's the gospel truth,' Elliot whined. 'Me and Buzz weren't privy to Clinton's scheming. I reckon his opining to raid another homestead, all his boys were getting armed up when me and Buzz left town.'

Elliot gave Will an assaying look to see if there was a slight chance of swinging things his way. He couldn't see any. The black muzzle hole of the Colt stared back at him like some evil eye, unmoving, shit-scary. One wrong move and he'd end up like poor Buzz with the back of his head blown away. Silently he vented his fear and frustrated anger on Phil Clinton for sticking him out on this creaking limb.

'You're lucky I ain't a vindictive man,' Will said. 'So I ain't about to send you down to hell to meet up with your buddy, though you sure deserve to join him. Just step down, easy like, and unbuckle your gunbelt then load him on to his horse and get to hell out of this valley and stay out or you'll definitely get plugged if I meet up with you again. The money you both got for this chore should see your pal decently buried.'

While Elliot was strapping Buzz's body on his horse Will drew both rifles out of their boots. He gave Elliot a hard-faced grin. 'Just in case you get tempted to throw-down on me with a long gun when you ride off a piece. Though to do so would get you dead, pilgrim. I've a big Sharps 50 back there in the barn. I'd blow you clear off your horse even if you were halfway to Plainsville.'

Elliot, opining that it wasn't his day for dying, gave Will a daring fierce, we'll get-even, scowl as he mounted his horse. When the widow woman and three kids stepped out on to the porch, the kids hardly strong enough to hold the rifle and pistols they were aiming at him, Elliot's stomping man's look cracked and he almost burst into tears. Him and Buzz had been conned. The kids couldn't have hit a barn door. If he'd backed Buzz's play the pair of them could have taken the homesteader. It was too late now to try and alter the situation. He hadn't a cat in hell's chance of facing the hard-faced bastard in a one to one pistol fight and ending up alive, even if his pistol wasn't already beaded on him. Elliot took hold of the reins of Buzz's mount then fiercely dug his spurs into his horse's ribs and headed back to Plainsville. And to have strong words with that Missouri backshooter, Mr Phil Clinton.

Will eyed Elliot till he had dropped out of sight behind a rise in the trail, and a while longer in case the would-be raider did try and push his luck by swinging round to come ass-kicking on in, pistol blazing away. Only then did he go back into the barn and pick up the Sharps and join Meg and her children on the porch.

Darkness was closing in fast, the Mc-Dowell boys were lighting the lamps in the shack while Meg and her daughter prepared the evening meal. Will, standing on the porch, gazing unseeingly into the night, wondered if he could take the saddletramp's word that Phil Clinton and his Missourians were going to do their dirty work elsewhere in the valley. The prime location he plumped for was Mr Ira Brook's homestead. The way old Jake had figured the marauders' leader would react when he found out about the killing of his three men.

Meg came out on to the porch and sensing what was passing through Will's mind she said, 'If you want to go and see if any of the other valley folk need help you go, Will. We'll be fine here now. Didn't that man say that the raiders won't be coming here.'

Will turned and faced her. 'It's a bar-rat's word we're takin', Meg.'

'I'm willing to trust him,' Meg replied. 'If you feel that you're beholden to go, Will, then you go. You said it was the whole valley's fight. Other homesteaders will be in as great a danger as I am.'

'Mr Ira Brooks is,' Will said. 'It will be his place Mr Phil Clinton and his wild bunch will be making for.' He then told Meg about the killing of the three occupiers of Ira's shack.

Meg's hands flew to her mouth in alarm. 'Then you must go, Will,' she cried. 'You should have stayed with him instead of coming here.'

'Mr Brooks agreed that I should come here,' Will said. He smiled at Meg. 'He said that he was more than capable of holding off a bunch of Missouri white trash.'

'I'll get the boys to saddle up your horse,' Meg said. 'While you come indoors and have something to eat or at least a drink of coffee.' Meg's face took on a sober look. 'You could be too busy where you're going to bother about meals.'

Meg, putting a hand on his arm, stopped Will with one foot in the stirrup and his other leg poised to swing into his saddle. Then to his pleasant surprise Meg kissed him on the cheek. 'You will take care, won't you?'

Will smiled. 'I'm a middle-aged sodbuster, Meg. Not some howlin'-at-the-moon young hellion. Cautious is my middle name.'

Meg smiled back at him. 'I wouldn't have guessed it, Mr Harding. We will see you again, won't we?'

'You can bank on it, Mrs McDowell,' Will replied. 'I'll make it my business to see that you're not left on your own to fight this trouble. M'be I'll even pay you a call after the fighting is all over.'

Meg's, 'I'd like that, Will,' ringing in his ears gave him some cheer on his ride to Ira's homestead. He clamped his jaw tight shut till his teeth ached. He was making a dangerous trip but if he wanted to see Meg McDowell again it would be Phil Clinton and his band of renegades that was making the dangerous trip by coming into the valley.

SEVEN

Ira, dozing in the wash, curled up in his blanket, heard his corralled horse's nervous snicker and became fully awake. His alarm hadn't worked, the sons-of-bitches were in real close. The few minutes breathing space he had lost because his alarm signalling-rifle had failed temporarily threw him in a panic. Quickly getting a grip of his nerves he made a shield of his blanket and thumbed a match into flame and lit the lantern before putting the match to the fuse of one of the sticks of blasting powder.

He tossed the lantern at the oil-soaked brush, heard its glass shatter on impact, and the roaring whoosh of flames as the brush burst into a fast running line of fire. Just on the edge of the flickering light the flames cast, Ira saw a bunch of men on foot, the reason he fleetingly opined, for their silent approach, scattering like bats disturbed by torchlight. With a wide over-arm lob he flung the stick of dynamite at them, its red spluttering fuse only two inches in length.

It exploded in a blinding flash almost as it hit the ground and Ira thought that he heard a sharp cry of pain mingled in the noise of the explosion. He hadn't time to listen for more cries to find out if it had been for real or fanciful thinking on his part. He brought his rifle up on to the rim of the wash and tried to pinpoint any of the men the blast had sent running for cover. They were real enough. He hadn't long to wait for the raiders to fight back. A rifle flashed near the corral, then two more right and left of it. Further away two more rifle muzzles flared red in the dark. All firing at the shack. Ira gave a tight-faced smile. He'd well and truly shook up the sons-of-bitches.

He fired off the full load of the Winchester, punching single spread shots along the corral fencing. He got the satisfaction after he'd finished firing of noticing that only four rifles were in action there now. He dropped the rifle and ran, crouched low, along the wash to his second firing position, leaving behind him the dirt where he'd been standing kicked feet high by the heavy barrage of retaliatory fire. His small battle, Ira thought, had been joined with a vengeance.

Ira picked up the second rifle but before bringing it into use he tried to anticipate the marauder leader's next move, him knowing where he was and that only one rifle had been firing. What would make them a little hesitant in closing in for the kill, Ira opined, would be that they didn't know how much dynamite he had. As far as they knew he could have a whole box full of the stuff, capable of blowing all of them clear out of the State of Kansas.

Five rifles were laying down a heavy curtain of lead along the wash and Ira did a quick mental count of the marauders' losses. The seven rifles he'd first counted plus the man he reckoned to have knocked out with the blasting stick made eight raiders. Take him and the man that had ceased firing at the corral off, and the gang was down to six men. But only five rifles were firing at him? Had he put two of them out of action with the dynamite? Then alarm bells rang loudly in Ira's ears. The rifle fire was covering the owner of the rifle he couldn't account for. The bastard was belly-crawling towards the wash. It was time for the second stick of dynamite.

Ira lit the fuse and again let it burn well down to prevent the stick being picked up by some fast-thinking marauder and slung back at him and flung it in the direction of the riflemen. Midway between them and the wash. Ira's calculating guess paid off. The split second red flaming centre of the earth raising explosion framed a black figure, arms and legs threshing wildly, cartwheeling in midair, landing somewhere beyond the now burnt-out line of brush.

Ira gripped his rifle tighter and peered

wide-eyed into the darkness. Now it was only five to one. Still formidable odds. He couldn't bank on Lady Luck running his way much longer. If they closed in on him he'd have little or no chance of holding them at bay. Before that even happened he'd try and regain the advantage by putting the second part of his defence plan into action; leaving the shelter of the wash and circle in on the marauders for a final shootout with fast-firing pistol to shorten the odds still further. If that failed, cut and run for it, if he was still able to, and fight another day. Come daylight if he stayed in the wash he would stay there forever, dead.

Ira fired off the remainder of the Winchester loads just to fool them that he was still there and prepared to make a fight of it. Dropping the rifle he picked up the spare pistol and moved slowly and silently along the wash to the bend where it deepened before it climbed away from his holding. It was deep enough for him to stand upright without the risk of getting his head blown off. He could no longer see the rifle flashes but as far as he could judge from the sounds of the firing, the marauders had fallen for his con. He could hear no shells whizzing over his part of the wash.

Ira's hair on the back of his neck began to bristle – a self-warning signal the war years had unconsciously developed, a seventh sense. He stopped and listened hard.

In the short silences between the rifle reports he heard a slight grating sound in the darkness along the wash ahead of him, like a foot slipping on a patch of shale. One of the bastards had sneaked into the wash. Ira's throat dried up. He pulled out his own pistol and slowly cocked the hammers of both weapons and waited. Half-crouched, teeth bared in a fighting dog-like snarl. Ira didn't think too deeply that another man, more Indian-footed, could be coming along the wash behind him.

At first he sensed rather than saw a dark blurred shape moving towards him. He allowed the marauder to come in close, near enough to hear him curse softly as he stumbled over some obstacles on the floor of the wash before he fired.

The twin barrel flashes vividly lit up a fear-startled, open-mouthed face, the pistol cracks drowning out the marauder's death cry. Ira scrambled out of the farside of the wash and flung himself to the ground, his pistols pointing down into the wash, waiting for the marauders' next move. He guessed that they would be wondering what the outcome of the shots they had heard in the wash was. He'd wait till they knew for certain that their buddy had lost out for keeps before he started on the offensive again.

Phil Clinton was running out of moves. He was running out of boys. He didn't need it written in big whitewash letters on the side of a barn what the two pistols shots meant. Bill had been toting a rifle. The son-of-a-bitch had done for him. Who the hell was it down there in that wash? The wild-ass had downed four of his boys. Why, the blue bellies during the war hadn't killed as many of his men in so short a time. He could burn the shack down but a few burning timbers wouldn't satisfy his killing lust. Not till the man in the wash was gut shot or hanging by the neck under some tree would his blood count return to normal.

There was a self-preservation reason for not burning the shack down. To get near enough to torch it meant crossing seventy, eighty yards of open ground. A short but highly dangerous run, inviting another stick of dynamite to come their way. And he could ill afford losing any more of his gang. He would sit it out here, it was still four to one, waiting for daylight, or the sodbuster made a false move. Whichever, the sodbuster was dead, he'd guarantee it. If he didn't cut and run for it.

Will rode across the edge of Jake Mills' land. The shack's lamps were lit and all seemed quiet. Jake and his family, so far, were having a trouble-free night. Just then Will heard a muffled thud, too deep and resounding to be the discharge of even a heavy calibre rifle.

Well clear of Jacob's holding, Will heard another earth-vibrating boom and much fainter, the crackle of rifle fire. Ira's holding was under attack, and Will had the wild thought that the Missouri raiders had brought a fieldpiece with them to blow Ira out of his shack. He was all set to ass-kick his mount into a gallop when the drumbeat-sound of hard riding horses caused him to jerk his mount to a halt and twist round in his saddle, a hastily drawn pistol in his hand. Two riders loomed out of the dark-ness and Will drew back the pistol's hammer.

'It's me, Ben Mills, Mr Harding!' one of the riders called out before they reached Will. A relieved Will eased the hammer forward and sheathed the Colt as the two riders drew up alongside him. 'Me and Pat have been on watch,' Ben continued. 'Saw you cuttin' across Pa's land. Pa said that if we heard sounds of trouble from Mr Brooks' place me and Pat had to ride over there fast and help him out. We heard the blastin' sticks go off so here we are. I reckon that you've got the same notion in mind, Mr Harding. I guessed it was you bein' on your own and coming from the widow McDowell's direction.'

'Dynamite?' Will gasped incredulously.

Ben grinned. 'Yeah. Two sticks of it. Pa had them left over after blastin' out some tree roots on our land.'

'Well let's stop our jawin',' Will growled, 'and get ourselves across there. That's rifle fire I can hear. Mr Brooks has got a real war on his hands.'

Ira made certain that all the chambers in both pistols were loaded with live shells then with determination, tempered by natural fear, he slowly got to his feet. It was the darkest part of the night. The nocturnal hunters' time, the killing time. The fire from the remaining four marauders had only been spasmodic the last few minutes but more crucial to the success of his scheme, lengthening his chance of staying alive, none of them had changed their positions. It only needed him to move as silently as an Indian, and aim true. Not much, Ira thought dryly, considering the night was as black as the inside of a tar barrel and the odds didn't bear thinking about. The more he thought about what could be in store for him in the next few minutes, the more crazy his plan seemed.

Will picked out four rifles, firing he guessed in the direction of the wash he had used to come on to the shack unobserved. He couldn't see any answering fire from Ira but he reckoned that he was still alive or he wouldn't be drawing rifle fire, and played it right by not letting himself be trapped in his shack. Will looked harder but couldn't see any more rifle flashes. The hired gunman he'd got the drop on at Meg's shack had said that eight marauders were on the loose. That could mean that four of them were trying to outflank Ira before opening up, or Ira had

had a good killing time. There was another reason for the unaccounted-for raiders. One Will didn't want to contemplate. They could be raiding Meg's homestead. The quicker the raiders were driven off the sooner he'd find out where they were.

Will and the two boys dismounted and spaced themselves along the ridge. 'Don't get excited boys,' Will said as he thumbed a shell into the breech of the Sharps. 'It looks as though there's only four sonsuvbitches down there. They're hit-and-run men by trade not backs-to-the-wall fighters. When we open up they'll skedaddle to hell out of it, you'll see.'

Ira saw two rifles open up away to his left and flung himself to the ground. His determination suddenly shattered. The bastards had him boxed in. Where the hell had those two been when all the firing had been going on? Raiding another homestead? A third new rifle flamed and Ira sobbed aloud his relief. There could be only one big gun like that in the valley. Ex-Johnny Reb,

Mr Will Harding, had arrived to take a hand in the game. For the second time in as many days he'd come to pull him out of the shit, with his cannon and two much-needed reinforcements. Ira dropped back into the wash and joined in the firing. It was extreme range for accurate pistol firing though he reckoned still unnerving for the men he was firing at. And it would let Will know that he was still alive and fighting.

When the two rifles opened up on them Phil Clinton quickly decided that it was time to pull out what was left of his gang. The whole far ridge could soon be bristling with rifle-firing sodbusters. Blood revenge came second to the safety of his own hide. The bang of the big rifle and its slug splintering a corral fence post in two alongside him made that pull-out a full scale, belly-hugging dirt, panicky retreat to the timber and the horses.

Will raised a hand. 'OK boys,' he said. 'It looks as though we've licked them. They ain't firing any more. But stay low and keep a sharp lookout just in case the sonsuvbitches are only changing positions.'

Suddenly Will heard a single shot well away from where the marauders had been that puzzled him. It didn't puzzle Ira. He grinned. His trap had worked after all. He would soon find out if he'd netted anything. He got to his feet and yelled, 'It's OK, Mr Harding to come on down! Though watch out for the fellas I believe I only winged!'

A lamp had been brought from the shack and instructing Ben and Pat to stand on guard in case the marauders' withdrawal had been some sort of a trick, Ira and Will, pistols cocked, began to search for the casualties. A man groaning loudly attracted their attention first. The held high lantern shone on a man unsteadily raising himself from the ground. There was the darkness of a blood patch on his brow, but as far as they could see he didn't seem seriously hurt. Ira reckoned he had been knocked cold by the first dynamite blast. Will struck him on the head with his pistol barrel, which stopped his groaning and stretched him back on the ground again, dead to the world. He fierce-grinned Ira.

'That will keep the sonuvabitch out of our hair till we check on whoever else is lyin' out here.'

The still, shallow-breathing man lying in a crumpled heap at the corral was in a bad way. The Winchester's slug had caught him high in the chest, a killing wound, Ira clinically opined. He'd be lucky if he made it to Plainsville alive. Live tough, be prepared to die tough, Ira thought. The marauder was only getting his just deserts. The man he'd seen blown up was well and truly all broken-limbed dead. Ira didn't check on the raider in the wash. A man doesn't get up and walk away after receiving two Colt pistol shells in the face at pointblank range. Ira's trap had caught a victim. A broken-backed man lying under his shot dead horse.

Will let out a long low whistle. 'You're a one man army. It's no wonder we rebs lost the war. You've cut the gang down by over half.'

'As much as that?' said Ira. 'Well it was no great shootin' on my part, Mr Harding,' he added modestly. 'The stupid bastards asked to be shot or blown up. Do you know who they were?'

'Yeah,' replied Will. 'They're a gang of Missourian renegades bossed by a fella called Clinton. I met up with two saddle-bums that Clinton had hired to get Meg ... er ... Mrs McDowell off her land. Clinton wanted all his boys for stompin' on you. Though as it turned out he was wasting his time. One of the hired widow-frighteners told me all he knew about the gang. His pard, well, I had to shoot him. The sonuvabitch fancied his chance as a pistolero and lost out.'

'M'be the valley will get some peace now,' Ira said. 'Being the gang's all but wiped out.'

'I wouldn't bet on it,' Will said. 'The threat's still there. Clinton ain't no land-grabber. Someone is hiring him to do the dirty work. If whoever it is wants the valley real badly he'll give Clinton the go ahead to raise himself another bunch of Missouri hard–men.'

Ira did some deep-thinking before he spoke. 'We'll just have to catch up with this fella Clinton and persuade him to tell us who pays his wages, and why. Then we go after Mr Big himself. Or we can sit tight-assed with worry here waiting for them to come swooping down on the valley again.'

Will gave a tight-faced smile. 'I reckon we go after Clinton, Mr Brooks. It's the only option we've got. But first I'll wake up that fella I laid out and ask him to tell us all he knows about Clinton. Then he can take his wounded buddy to Plainsville to see the doc, if it ain't too late, or we'll have another grave to dig. We'll bring the two boys in to see the rest of them planted then they can go home. Their folks will be worrying about them. If that's OK with you, Mr Brooks.'

'Seems the thing to do, Mr Harding,' Ira replied.

Phil Clinton, face meaner-looking than ever,

vented the hate and anger that was boiling up inside him by digging his spurs savagely into his horse's flanks, drawing blood. In his dust-trail rode Vince and Joe, the last of the Clinton gang that could still ride a horse and fire a gun. Joe was wishing that he had caught a slug in his arm the same time Tex had. Then he could have stayed in Plainsville bouncing that plump-assed whore instead of having to eat dirt on some sodbuster's land waiting to be blown to bits like Sam, or plugged, as the other boys had been, m'be for keeps.

What brought the fear-sickness clawing at Joe's throat was the scary thought that it had only been one sodbuster who had brought all the mayhem. Christ, he thought, if they'd stayed on when the other three showed up none of them would be making it back to Plainsville, that was for sure. He'd tell Phil so, but not at this very moment or he'd get no nearer to that whore he fancied than where he was right now. He could see that Clinton was as mad as a hound dog with rabies. The son-of-a-bitch would gun him down in the blink of an eye if he raised one little protest about the wisdom of carrying on with the raiding now that the homesteaders in the valley were prepared to make a fight of it, and damn well winning.

Joe had judged Clinton's feelings right. Phil was mean-mad enough to shoot dead both Joe and Vince, and their horses, if they so much as gave him a leery-eyed look. He was a long way from quitting the fight. He was intending to continue on to Missouri to hire another bunch of Kansas-haters and come back to Big Creek valley and burn down everything that could burn – shacks, barns, every acre of growing crop. Kill anyone that stood in his way, women and kids included. Leaving the valley a burnt-out wasteland.

The dead had been decently buried, the unwounded and the wounded marauders sent on their way to Plainsville. Ben and Pat were thanked for their help and were ready to ride back to their homesteads, with the dead raiders' guns, to tell their folk about their victory over the raiders and Ira and Will's intentions to track down the last few members of the gang.

'I'd be obliged if you can still come and see to the chores on my place, and Mr Brooks, Ben, while we're both away,' Will said. He looked sheepishly at Ira before facing Ben again. 'And I'd consider it a real favour if you'd let the widow McDowell know that I'm OK and that I hope to see her when I get back from Plainsville and that she hasn't to fear the raiders any more.' Will fierce-eyed Ben. 'But don't tell her that it's a pistol-fightin' trip me and Mr Brooks are goin' on, understand?'

Ira could see that Ben, like he, was trying hard not to smile at the thought of the hard-man, Mr William Harding, sparking up to the widow McDowell. But Ira wasn't going to ask how things were between him and the widow, he'd wait till Will felt that he had to tell someone about his affections for Mrs McDowell. Ira didn't want to start the war between the north and the south again.

'I'll do that, Mr Harding,' Ben said. 'And me and Pat will keep an eye on your place as well, Mr Brooks. You don't want us to go to Plainsville to give you a hand to put paid to the rest of the sonsuvbitches, Mr Harding?' Ben added eagerly.

Will gave a tight-lipped smile and shook his head. 'Thanks for the offer Ben, don't think it ain't appreciated, ain't that so, Mr Brooke?' Ira nodded his head in agreement. 'Your job,' Will continued, 'is to hold the line here in case me and Mr Brooks don't make it back. Then you might get more killin' than you can stomach. Now ride on out, boys, me and Mr Brooks have some packin' to do.'

EIGHT

It was long past noon before Ira and Will set off for their tracking down of the remnants of the Clinton gang, Plainsville being their first stop to pick up the marauders' trail. Will had returned to his holding for a few hours sleep before seeing to his chores and loading what rations he had in store onto a packhorse. Jangled-nerved as the reaction of the night battle set in, Ira only managed an hour or so of fitful, uneasy dozing. Filling in the time till Will returned by cleaning and reloading his guns, he then saddled up his horse, getting all ready for a quick move out.

'OK, Mr Brooks,' Will said. 'Let's ride, before the trail gets cold. Mr Clinton will opine by now that we have a fair idea of who's doin' the raidin' and we can give a description of some of his boys to the law at Plainsville, thereby fingerin' him, so I reckon he'll have moved on from Plainsville real fast to escape a hangin'. My bet he'll be haulin' his ass to Missouri to tell his paymaster what's happened. Then we'll have to expect the worst, another bunch of barn-burners to contend with.' Will close-eyed Ira. 'We'll have to walk softly and smile a lot once across the border, Mr Brooks. Old brush boys still have a lot of friends there.'

Ira grinned. 'I ain't nothin' but a poor ploughboy, mister.' His smile faded as he took a final look at his shack before swinging into his saddle. 'Sometime, Mr Harding,' he said, soberly, 'I might be able to stay in my home for a decent spell without having to leave it to go out and drive off some pesterin' assholes.'

'M'be, if we get real lucky,' Will answered, 'it could be pretty soon.'

As they cut on to the main trail they both saw the dust of a wagon being driven at speed coming towards them. They drew up their mounts.

'Someone is in a helluva hurry, Mr Harding,' Ira said.

'Sure is,' replied Will. 'I hope it ain't bad news. They reckon that travels fast. Well I'll be ... it's Meg!' He shot an embarrassed glance at Ira. 'Er ... the widow, Mrs McDowell.'

Straight-faced, hiding his inner smile, Ira said, 'She ain't lashing that mule like a Missouri mule skinner to pass the time of day with me, Mr Harding.' Leaning over he took the packhorse's lead rope out of Will's hand. 'You hang back here and see what it's all about, I'll ride ahead, you can catch me up.' Ira tongue-clicked his horse into a walk, leaving Will standing there before he could say otherwise. Looking over his shoulder he saw that Will had swung his horse round to ride along the trail to meet up with the wagon. Will touched his hat in a greeting as Meg drew up the wagon, trying not to show the worry he was feeling about her unexpected appearance. Meg soon put him at ease.

'Ben told me that you and Mr Brooks were making a trip to Plainsville, Will,' she said. 'I thought that you might need some rations, coffee, beans, and some newly baked bread.' She smiled hesitantly. 'If ... if you're away any length of time it will save you buying rations at Plainsville. It's the least I can do after all you've done for me and my family.'

Under her breath the widow McDowell asked for the Lord's forgiveness for telling a lie, albeit a small lie, without any malice or intent to deceive. She had wheedled out of Ben (in fact Ben was bursting with excitement to tell her of his part in the fight) the frightening news of the killings at Mr Brooks' shack. The so-called trip was only the continuation of that battle. Only this time Will, and Mr Brooks, might not come out of it as the victors. Meg was aware that she was acting like a schoolgirl having a first crush on a boy, not like a widow woman with a family. But she couldn't help it. She just had to see Mr Harding again however he may feel towards her – to grab a few more minutes of the sweetness he had brought into her life – which since the death of her man and her boy had been a sad and bitter time. And the way things were shaping up in the valley, the raiding, the killings, life could get even tougher for her and her family.

'Why thank you, Meg,' Will said as he took the offered package of supplies. 'It's real thoughtful of you. They'll come in real handy.' Which wasn't altogether true. He'd loaded the packhorse with more rations than he'd lived on for nigh on two weeks when fighting with the Jackson brigade in the Shenandoah campaigns. That didn't mean that he wasn't pleased to see Meg, doubly so knowing that she wanted to see him – wisely opining that the bringing of the rations was only an excuse. Even hard men like him craved a little happiness in their lives sometimes. More than he'd dared hope, in so short a relationship, the widow Meg McDowell was doing just that.

'You will take care,' Meg said, moist-eyed with concern.

Will smiled comfortingly. 'I already said I would, Meg, back at your place. And don't fret none about Mr Brooks leading me into any trouble. Why, he's more peaceably inclined than me. He'd ride a half a day's journey just to avoid trouble.'

Meg's eyes flashed angrily. 'Mr Harding you are the biggest liar in the whole valley. You should have been a big city lawyer. Young Ben told me about all that happened here last night. I just pray that the pair of you don't meet some real trouble that's all.' Then, her anger vanishing as fast as it came, she said, 'I had no right to speak the way I did, please forgive me. You're only doing what you think's right. My man did that ... it got him dead...' Meg's voice broke and she couldn't trust herself even to look at Will or she would have burst into tears. She tugged at the reins, turning the wagon and drove back along the trail. Only then did she let loose of her emotions and the tears flowed warm and salty down her cheeks.

Will caught up with Ira, Meg's obvious concern for him still softening his features.

'Everything OK, Mr Harding?' asked Ira.

'Yeah ... yeah,' replied Will. 'Mrs McDowell brought us some rations that's all. She's OK.'

'She seems a fine woman,' Ira said.

'She sure is, Mr Brooks.' Ira saw Will's face change, become wild-eyed, hard-planed. 'And I'll gut shoot any Missouri brush boy from here to the border rather than see her or her family come to any harm.'

And Ira thought he was mighty glad that he'd never met up with Mr Harding in his present frame of mind during the war.

NINE

Elliot had left Buzz's body, still strapped across his horse, outside the undertaker's parlour, a five-dollar bill stuck in a dead claw-like hand. Elliot didn't want to be linked too closely to the dead Buzz, bringing the unwelcome possibility of being asked awkward questions by the marshal on just how Buzz had got himself shot. The tin-badge man might then take it into his head to have another look at his old wanted flyers and come across his and Buzz's likenesses on one of them and he would end up on the rock-pile in the State pen.

Elliot was chewing on another slight problem as he rode on to the livery barn – how to explain to Phil Clinton of his failure to get a widow woman and her three kids off her land. Phil wasn't the happiest of men to do business with and it wouldn't make him any more cheerful knowing that he had paid out hard cash for a job not done. But Elliot felt that failure or not, he was entitled to hang on to the payment for the risk he'd taken. And wasn't Buzz already spending some of his cut? Elliot's face firmed up. Why, he'd tell the weasel-faced bastard that he'd steered him wrong, the widow woman hadn't been on her ownsome. Laying it on real thick he'd tell of a gun fight with at least four or five sodbusters. Buzz lying stiff on a board in the undertaker's parlour would silently but convincingly back him up.

Satisfied that Phil could not have any comeback on him, Elliot unsaddled his horse then walked across to the saloon – to have a good drink and later a woman and to celebrate the fact that he was still able to partake in the pleasures of the flesh. It was a bleary-eyed, still half-drunk, pants hanging loosely about his waist, Elliot, that staggered across the back lot to the crapper a little after dawn and saw Phil, Vince and Joe coming into town. His fuzzy-headiness vanished as he read the looks on their faces. They'd had their asses well and truly burnt, and he stopped wondering where the rest of the gang were. His tale about the big pistol fight at the widow's place would sound all the more real.

Suddenly Elliot realized that Clinton wouldn't be in the right frame of mind to take another helping of bad news. He'd leave it till later, when Clinton had some whisky inside him, mellowing him somewhat. As much as a man who earned his living by killing and burning down homesteads could soften.

'Get what you want from your rooms,' Clinton said, as they drew up outside the rooming house. 'Then we'll push on to Two Forks before those sodbusters ride into Plainsville to finish off what they started back there in the valley. Or get the Marshal to serve warrants on us. If any of the boys we left there are alive they can finger us. I'll leave you both at Two Forks while I ride on to Jackson City and get the big man to tip out some more cash so that I can raise me another bunch of gunhands. Tex can stay here, the sodbusters can't finger him as being on the raid. He can keep his ears open for any news the sodbusters may be planning next.'

By noon Elliot felt that he had held off long enough from facing Clinton. He was also curious to know just what the hell had happened to the rest of the gang in Big Creek valley. Furthermore he had the pressing urge to partake in the hair of the dog that had bitten him last night. Pushing open the swing doors of the Plainsville saloon, Elliot, after a quick glance round, could only see Tex, arm still strapped up in a dirty white sling, bellied up to the bar. He walked over to him and ordered a whisky. He cast an over-the-shoulder glance at the gaming tables at the rear of the saloon but still couldn't see any more members of the Clinton gang.

'Where's Phil? I saw him, Vince and Joe ride into town,' he said. 'They weren't exactly shoutin' for joy. And where's the rest of the boys? Did they meet trouble in the valley? Me and Buzz sure did. It got Buzz dead.'

'They met trouble all right, one hundred percent, gold-plated trouble,' Tex said. 'A while back Cal rode in with Pete tied across his horse, shot real badly. The croaker reckons he's on a one-way trip to Boot Hill before the day's out. Cal told Phil that the other three boys are already dead so Phil, and what's left of the gang, are headin' for Two Forks just in case the sodbusters come into town huntin' for them. I'm stayin' on here, can't ride in case my wound opens up, and not being on the raid, I'm in the clear. Phil says he'll pick me up when he comes back. I ain't keen on goin' out raidin' again but you know how Phil is.'

Elliot began to sweat and ran a finger round the inside of his collar. He wished now he'd kept on riding. Missouri m'be.

The sodbusters knew he was tied up with the Clinton gang. One of them had let him go, the others might not be so charitably inclined. If they came into town he could end up alongside Buzz. He ordered another whisky to try and stop his shakes and sweats.

Ira and Will eased pistols in holsters as they left the livery barn to begin their hunt for the raiders, or pick up news of their whereabouts. Their first choice was the Plainsville saloon, the hangout of the gang. They had ridden into Plainsville at dusk – it didn't do to act carelessly and let themselves be seen by the opposition, if still in town, and lengthen the already dangerous odds.

'I'll keep an eye out for that fella Clinton sicced on to Mrs McDowell,' Will said. 'I might be able to pump him some more. As I said I think Clinton and what's left of his gang will have quit town.' Will favoured Ira with a humourless smile. 'If I'm wrong there's at least one of the sonsuvbitches know who we are so we throw down on anyone that so much as gives us a fish-eyed look.'

Elliot saw them come into the saloon. The man he hadn't seen before was, in his expert opinion, a younger version of the stone-eyed, fast shooting bastard who had killed Buzz. A man Elliot inspiringly thought capable of killing half of Phil Clinton's gang. Elliot's backbone stiffened up, the old bastard wasn't going to make him eat crow again, and worse. In his mind's eye he saw the hanging rope. Face twisted in an angry defiant snarl of the desperate courage of a next-to-no-chance man, he grabbed for his pistol.

Stone cold sober, Elliot would have been downright foolish to make a stand against men with combat experience and finely honed reactions to danger. Still carrying a hangover, Elliot's pride had pushed him real close to the doorway of hell.

Ira and Will saw the blurred movement at the far end of the bar and their hands sped smoothly to their guns. The two slugs smacked hard into Elliot's chest, their discharges sounding as one extra loud crack and Elliot was on his way to meeting up with Buzz in hell. Half-crouched, shoulder to shoulder, Ira and Will swept the pistols in a slow, menacing arc across the drinkers at the bar. Seeing no further hostile movement against them they relaxed, straightening up and easing the pistol hammers forward slipped the Colts back into their sheaths.

'You all saw him draw first, folks,' Will said. 'For no damn reason at all. Me and my pard were just coming in for a drink.' Will had no intention of broadcasting the real reason of his and his pard's trip to Plainsville.

The bar came to life again, customers talking, drinking and watching a barkeep pick up Elliot by the shoulders and pull him out of the bar. Will and Ira strode across to the counter and ordered drinks. After the barkeep had put a bottle of whisky and two glasses in front of them he moved quickly to the other end of the bar, not wishing to be in the line of fire if any more of his customers fancied drawing on the two strangers. Will brought his glass up to take a drink but before he did so he said, 'Keep an eye through the bar mirror on that fella where the barkeep's standing, the one with his arm in a sling. The fella we just shot told me when I had him by the balls at Mrs McDowell's that there was a wounded marauder in town. Of course there could be more than one man in town with a bandaged-up arm but the way he keeps looking our way makes me opine that the bastard is one of Mr Phil Clinton's bunch.'

'Do we drag him along to the Marshal's office, Mr Harding, and sign a warrant for his arrest?' Ira asked.

'No,' replied Will. 'That will show our hand to any friends of Clinton in town, or Clinton himself if he's whoopin' it up somewhere else. If he leaves the saloon we'll follow him and have a quiet man to man palaver with him. Then we'll take him along to the jailhouse.' Will grinned. 'Meanwhile,

119

Mr Brooks, keep giving him the evil eye. Let him know we've got him sized up. It might make him quit drinking here sooner than he intended.'

Tex gripped his glass tight as though that was all that was preventing him from falling to the floor. He had heard Elliot's dying sigh as he fell against him and that blood-chilling sound had stopped him thinking of pulling out his own gun and backing Elliot's play. Apprehensively he looked at Elliot's killers through the mirror. The bastards knew that he rode with Clinton, they were just making him sweat. Tex's teeth clamped shut as tight as his fingers were on the glass as he waited for them to come in his direction, pistols out and firing. He almost felt the split second of agony that Elliot had felt when the Colt loads tore into him.

To his surprise, and extreme relief, the two sodbusters finished their drinks and walked out of the saloon, though not before giving him a last hard glance. Tex couldn't remember finishing his drink but on looking down he saw that his glass was empty. Weak-kneed, as though he had been with a woman twice over, he pulled himself away from the bar. One thing he was certain of, he was getting to hell out of Plainsville but fast. He would risk bleeding to death on the trail rather than stand here, crapping himself, waiting to be called out to face certain death by those two pistol-wielding sons-of-bitches, or the town marshal hauling him off to a necktie party.

Tex sneaked out of the saloon by the rear entrance and in no time at all he was entering the livery barn with his belongings bundled under his good arm to saddle his horse and ride out of Plainsville. Ira and Will stepped out from one of the stalls, smiling unkindly at him, pistols showing. 'Jesus H Christ,' he gasped, and his gear dropped from nerveless fingers.

'You tell us where that no-good murderin' sonuvabitch, Phil Clinton is, pilgrim?' Will snarled, as he jabbed Tex in the belly with his pistol. 'And don't give us any crap about you don't know who I'm talkin' about. We know the man that put that slug in your shoulder.'

Tex ran his tongue over dry lips, his shifty-eyed gaze darting from Will then to Ira. He tried to see any signs of mercy or bluffing on the expressionless, Indian-looking faces, but couldn't detect a gleam of either. Tex then thought that part truth was better than playing dumb and risk making the sons-of-bitches meaner than they were right now.

'Yeah, I used to ride with Clinton,' he said, 'but not since I got this busted shoulder. I've not seen him or the boys for a coupla days. They could be anywhere in the territory, m'be across in Missouri. I don't rightly know, mister.'

'Think harder, real harder, friend,' Will said, punctuating his words by prodding Tex's belly again with the pistol.

'You're wastin' your breath, Mr Harding, sweet-talking to the bastard,' Ira growled. 'Let's hang him and be done with it then we can try and pick up Clinton's trail ourselves.' Swinging his arm he threw one end of the rope he was carrying over the hay hoist bar. It slipped off at his first attempt and recoiling the rope he tried again. This time he was successful. He spat on his hands and pulled at the rope till the noose at the other end dangled five, six feet from the ground. 'All set,' he said. 'Bring the sonuvabitch over here, Mr Harding.'

A white, fear-contorted Tex watched with fascinated horror at the noose as it swung ominously before his eyes. He tried to make a run for it but Will clutched him tightly in a bear-like hug. Tex struggled frantically to free himself from Will's grip. His struggle to keep control of his body functions was just as futile and he felt the warm wetness at his groin spreading down his legs.

'Clinton and the boys are holed up at Two Forks near the Missouri border!' he screeched, his voice as high-pitched as a hysterical girl's. 'Clinton ain't stopping there though, he's riding across into Missouri ... Jackson City, he's business with a man there!'

'How many backshooters has he with him?' questioned Will.

'Three! Cal, Vince and Joe!' Tex cried. He didn't tell the two bastards that wanted to string him up what had happened to the rest of the gang. Like Elliot he'd bet that it was a sure certainty that not only did they know but they were the ones that did the shooting.

'Who's this man that Clinton's meeting up with in Jackson City?' Will said. 'Is he the man that wants the valley? Willing to pay assholes like you to do the killin' and the burnin'?'

'I don't know his name, mister, honest I don't,' Tex sobbed, still eyeing the noose. 'Clinton is the only man that deals with him. All I know he wants the valley real bad and is willing to pay well to see that he gets it. And I swear to God I don't know any more!'

Will close-eyed the marauder. He seemed scared enough to have been speaking the truth. 'OK, mister,' he said. 'I believe you.' He turned to Ira. 'What do we do with him, Mr Brooks? If we take him along to the Marshal there'll be papers to sign, that's if we find the Marshal in his office. He'll probably be doing his nightly rounds. All that will take time and we don't want Clinton's trail to get any colder than it is right now.'

Ira winked at Will, then scowling at Tex he said, 'Hang him, I say. I've got myself real worked up for a hangin'.'

Tex found that he hadn't quite emptied his bladder and the dark patch at the front of his pants spread.

'Now, now, Mr Brooks,' chided Will. 'There's no need to be so uncharitable. He's told us what he knows. Let him go I say.' He cold-eyed Tex. 'But if we see him sneakin' along our back trail to try and warn Clinton of our coming then you can hang him, Mr Brooks, and I'll give you a hand on the rope.'

'Mister!' Tex blurted out, still high-pitched

voiced. 'I'm finished with the Clinton gang! I swear on my mother's grave I'll give you no more trouble!' He gave Ira a pleading hound dog look.

'It goes against my better judgement, Mr Harding,' Ira said as he jerked the rope off the bar and began coiling it up. 'But I'll take the sonuvabitch's word, I wouldn't like to sell his ma short, she could have been a good woman. Though I'll be riding with my head screwed round and if I see so much as...'

'You won't,' said Tex. 'Why ... why, I'd shoot my horse here and now just to prove that I ain't about to trail you!'

'There ain't no need to make a poor innocent horse pay for your evil ways of earning your keep,' Will said. 'You just go back into the saloon and continue with your drinking and contemplate on how you've seen the Light. Of course, being careful men, Mr Brooks here will keep an eye on the saloon. We ain't leaving town till morning,' he lied, 'so if he sees you leave the saloon and head for any other place but where you're bedded down, he'll plug you for keeps. You'll have cottoned on by now that Mr Brooks is one mean sonuvabitch. Now go and change your pants, it ain't fit and proper for a grown man to stand at a bar wearing piss-soaked pants.'

Tex didn't need telling twice. Hastily he grabbed up his gear, using his wounded arm as well, not worrying about it starting to bleed again, in his eagerness to escape the mad-crazy kid and his hanging rope.

After he'd gone Will and Ira burst out laughing. 'What would you've done, Mr Brooks, if the fella had called our bluff by keeping his mouth shut?'

'I never doubted that he wouldn't crack, Mr Harding,' Ira replied. 'Your face ain't what's called a homely, friendly type of face. I imagine he was seeing feathers sticking out of your hair and scalps hanging from your belt. My noose only made him make his mind up that little bit faster. Now let's ride out while the bastard's still shit-scared.'

Any gawking passer-by on the trail would have catalogued Ira and Will as back-country hicks, harmless drifters. Not hair-trigger men bent on a vengeance trail, a kill or be killed mission. He would only see the booted rifle each of them had. More essential for any rider crossing the great plains than the wearing of pants. A man couldn't fend off hostiles by waving his pants in their faces. Bare-assed naked, but holding a long gun, he was more likely to hold on to his scalp.

Hidden from the casual eye was the single pistol tucked in the back of pants tops, covered from sight by buttoned up jackets and the extra pistol each had in a jacket pocket. If they had been told right, there were three men ahead of them, one knowing who they were. Dangerous, fast-shooting men. Men to take no chances with. Unshaven for days, hats pulled well down to hide their features, and no signs of a pistol belt, Ira and Will were hoping that they could get in close enough to the men they were seeking. To get the drop on them before they discovered that the unarmed country boys were really curly wolves out for their blood.

Both admitted that as far as plans went it didn't have much going for it but it was the best they could come up with. Time wasn't on their side. The longer they failed to corner Clinton the more time it gave him to build his gang anew. It wasn't the most agreeable of situations trying to get the better of men who by their lawless ways were highly suspicious and fast reaction men. Men who believed in shooting first and doing the talking later, if it was still necessary to do so.

'Remember, Mr Brooks,' warned Will before they'd cleared the outskirts of Plainsville. 'If any sonuvabitch gives us so much as an unkind look, draw on him. We're more than likely walking into a Daniel's den.'

TEN

Madame Isabel Depardieu, Frenchy Belle, drawing on a thin, brown cigarillo, stood on the balcony of what she boasted as being the best whorehouse in east Kansas, watching the two strangers getting off their horses outside Tate's livery barn. Out of habit she gave them the once over. Her years of working in, then owning, a bawdy house, had given her the expertise in being able to judge men's characters, the whole gambit of what made them tick.

No-good murdering assholes like Phil Clinton who had ridden out of town last night were easily read. Their vicious meanness showed in their faces and every time they opened their rat-trap mouths. The two newcomers to town puzzled her. They looked like genuine, easy come, easy go, country boys but she knew that half the killers in the territory had straw sprouting out of their ears. But while the wild boys had one, maybe two, big Colt pistols sheathed on well-filled refill belts that bagged their pants about their bellies, these were unarmed.

Yet she noticed that the glances the pair were casting about them lingered a little longer on who or what they were looking at. In her considered opinion more assessing than curious eyeballing of a new town they'd ridden into. Not that there was much to arouse anyone's interest in a dead-dog place like Two Forks, unless they'd come to pay her girls a visit. Frenchy Belle was foxed for the moment – she couldn't quite label them till she saw the bulge of a pistol stuck in the back of the older man's pants as his coat was rucked up when he swung out of his saddle.

Frenchy Belle swore. It looked like trouble was due to hit Two Forks. Unless what or who the pair seemed to be searching for had moved on. She looked more closely at the two men – unshaven and stern rather than hard-faced, especially the one whose gun she'd seen, and not showing the tight mean-mouthed scowl of a hired gun. They could be lawmen, she thought, then swore again. That would be worth writing home about, the law coming to Two Forks. She hoped that any trouble that might be about to burst on the town stayed out in the street or the saloons rather than in her place.

She'd never had big trouble in her house. There'd been the occasional normal fist fight when two half-drunken horn dogs came to blows over each wanting to pleasure the same girl first. Even during the war years, before in fact, when Quantrill's bloodthirsty boys were raising hell in the Kansas border lands. Putting the township of Lawrence to the torch, killing and looting not two hundred yards from where she was standing, the whorehouse hadn't been attacked. Frenchy Belle smiled. Why, her girls had satisfied the Missouri ragged-assed bush boys and John Brown's crackpot abolitionist zealots. Reb and blue belly soldier boys. She supposed that even men that took a delight in killing and burning down homesteads had the need of a woman from time to time.

There must have been some sort of an assholes' agreement, Belle opined – she didn't class the marauders, pro-reb Border Ruffians or Colonel Lane's Unionist Red Legs as gentlemen, – between the warring factions not to put her whorehouse to the torch. Or where else would the wild-asses go to get laid? Frenchy Belle took a final drag at her cigarillo before flicking it over the balcony rail. As she turned to go back into her room, she glimpsed the younger of the two strangers smiling and raising his hat to her. Heard him call out, 'You're the purtiest sight I've seen in a long day's ride, ma'am.'

Frenchy Belle walked back to the banisters. Being nobody's fool she knew it had been a long time since she'd been pretty. Though she'd thickened out here and there, sagged in other places, Frenchy Belle reckoned when she was all painted up, powdered and corsetted and wearing her best, she was still a fine figure of a woman, but no way pretty. In her negligee, see-through wrap, everything hanging loose, hair mussed up, she knew goddamned well she was anything but pretty. Angrily she looked down at her young praiser but saw no signs of mockery in the bearded face. Softening somewhat she smiled and waved a ring bedecked hand. 'Why thank you, kind sir, I trust that you will pay my establishment a visit later? Just tell the girls that you're Frenchy ... er, Madame Depardieu's special guest.'

'We ain't come to Two Forks to pleasure women,' Will said testily after Frenchy Belle had gone indoors.

'Think, Mr Harding,' said Ira, 'of what's the best and safest way to pick up news of Clinton and his boys. Poke our heads in every saloon asking barkeeps if they're acquainted with a Mr Phil Clinton and his band of cutthroats? Why, the first saloon we walk into we could come face to face with that fella we sent back to Plainsville with his shotup buddy. Then we'd have a pistol fight on our hands. That kind of barging-in approach tactics could get us dead.' Ira grinned. 'No wonder you rebs lost the war. We have to move as though we're striding across eggs.'

'Yeah, I reckon you've got a point there, Mr Harding,' said Will, dourly. 'How do you suggest we play, General?'

Ira pointed to the whorehouse. 'Those girls in there will have heard talk from men who normally wouldn't speak more than six words in a whole day, half of them grunts. That big bouncered madam, Frenchy, some name or another, will know everything about everybody in town. If I get real friendly with her I...'

'You can mix business with pleasure,' interrupted a now smiling Will.

'M'be, Mr Harding, m'be,' replied Ira. 'She's sure worth it.'

'It could work at that,' Will agreed. 'If we split up I can stay out of sight on the street. M'be I'll get lucky and see that fella we know.' Will gave a toothy, wolf's grin. 'Then you do your fish-eyed hangin' rope scene again to get him to give us a description of the other two assholes that's supposed to be in Two Forks.'

Cal, Joe, and Vince were sitting round a nearly empty bottle of Redeye in the Border saloon, contemplating their future. It had been an unanimous decision that they were not going back raising hell in the Big Creek valley. Not even if Clinton came back from his meeting with the big man in Jackson City with a bag of gold for each of them. As Cal had put it, a whole feed sack full of the yellow stuff was no good to a man all mashed up by a blasting stick going off under him.

'What we need, boys,' Cal said. 'Is a grubstake so that we can be far away from this dog shit town when Phil gets back, m'be

136

as far south as Texas. But I reckon that between us right now we couldn't put enough dough on this table for one of us to pay a visit to Frenchy Belle's.'

Vince and Joe were in total agreement with Cal's statement. They didn't want to tell Phil to his face that they wanted out. Otherwise the only trip they would be making would be on a fast, non-stopping train to hell. Robbing the town bank to get hold of the wherewithal for their journey south was a non-starter. Open or closed the bank was guarded by four special deputies armed with shotguns. It would take a full gang of ten, twelve men and a pitched battle to grab the bank's cash deposits.

Cal slow-grinned and put his glass down. 'I know where we can raise us a grubstake with no sweat at all.'

'Where would that be, Cal?' asked Vince.

'Why just along the street, Frenchy Belle's place,' replied Cal. 'She don't bank her week's takin's till tomorrow.' Cal's grin broadened into a real wide-eyed smile as the idea of taking the whorehouse madam's cash took hold. 'The money will be stashed away in some tin box in her room some place. A Colt stuck under her nose should soon make her tell us where.' He gave Vince and Joe a hard-eyed glance. 'OK? Boys, drink off and let's do it.'

ELEVEN

It was a slim, dark-haired girl, bare-footed, wearing only her drawers and a bodice hardly covering her well developed breasts, that led a round-eyed, admiring Ira up the stairs to Frenchy Belle's private room. The girl had told him that he was too early as most of the girls were still in bed asleep when he'd walked into the deserted hallway of the whorehouse.

Ira told her that he'd a special invite from Madame Isabel Depardieu to call on her. After giving him an eyebrow-raising, lip-twitching look, thinking that the old bitch's sap was rising early today, the girl told Ira to follow her. At the far end of the hall at the head of the stairs the girl stopped at a door and rapped on it with a knuckled hand. Behind the door Ira heard a voice call out,

'Who is it?'

Before his escort could answer he said, 'It's me, Madame Isabel. The fella that waved to you from the street, remember? You said if I called I had to ask for you.'

The dark-haired girl's eyebrows nearly reached her hairline with surprise – thinking that if every bum and saddletramp that waved to the boss got an invite to her room there'd be no work for the rest of the girls. It was a fully-dressed, ready to supervise the day's business, Madame Isabel Depardieu, that opened the door and asked Ira to step inside.

Frenchy Belle smiled at him. 'I'm just having coffee, would you care to join me, Mr ... er...?'

'Brooks, ma'am, Ira Brooks,' Ira said. 'And I wouldn't say no to a cup of your coffee.'

'Well just sit you down on that chair near the window, Mr Brooks, while I do the pouring. How do you like your coffee, Mr Brooks?'

'Just as it comes, ma'am,' Ira replied,

thinking that this close up Madame Isabel Depardieu was still a fine-looking female. He was handed a cup and saucer so delicately thin that he hardly dared hold them in case his fingers accidentally snapped the saucer in two. Uncomfortably he sat there, worried in case he broke Frenchy Belle's best china and feeling the pain of the Colt digging into his flesh every time he leaned back in the chair. Frenchy Belle's smile was no longer visible – she was now all hard-nosed businesslike.

'Now, you young asshole,' she said. 'What was all that horse shit, I was the prettiest thing you'd ever seen, for, eh? What do you want from me? Do you want a grubstake? One of my girls for free? Did you think that if you sucked up to me I'd go all girlish and soft-hearted? I've had real dandies, city gents, come that line, mister. You're welcome to the coffee but that's all you're getting. I only called you in to put things straight with you.'

Ira's face reddened and he felt the sting of

hot coffee on his thighs as his hands shook with the anger that had coloured his face. He put his cup down on to the floor and stood up. 'It ain't like as you say at all, ma'am. You did look real purty standing there in your flimsies and the sun shining on your hair and all. You still purty from where I'm standing right now, and that's the truth. I ain't looking for a handout or time with one of your girls for free, and that's another truth.'

'Sit down, boy,' Frenchy Belle said, 'or you'll bust a gut. Drink your coffee, I believe you.' She smiled again. 'But I know you young horn dogs, one day on the trail and anything that wears drawers is pretty. Thanks all the same. A woman that's getting on in years can't be too stuck-up-nosed not to accept a compliment when it's given honestly or otherwise.' Shrewd-eyeing him she said, 'Now you ain't climbed those stairs just to tell me how purty I look, have you, Mr Brooks? Or that you've a strong fancy to get me on to that bed?'

Ira sat down. A grin replaced the scowl on his face. 'It's been a long time since I did any bouncing, ma'am, being that I had other things on my mind such as preventing some Johnny Reb from killing me. And lately things ain't changed all that much for me.' He gave Frenchy Belle a long calculating look. He had to start asking some questions some time. That had to be weighed against Frenchy Belle's reactions to them. As he'd told Will, they were walking on eggs. He didn't want anyone else cracking them for them.

'You're right, ma'am,' he said. 'On one thing. I do want something from you but that in no way influenced my thinkin', how fine you looked out there on the balcony, and that's a fact. Me and my pard have come to Two Forks to seek out a Mr Phil Clinton and his boys. All we know about him is that he's a weasel-faced gent and at least he has three like-faced hombres with him. If you know anything at all about him, well I'd sure appreciate you telling me.'

143

It was Frenchy Belle's turn to spill coffee on her lap. Frozen faced with anger she snapped out, 'You ain't aiming to join up with that sonuvabitch, are you? If you are I had you figured wrong.'

Ira shook his head. 'No, ma'am, I ain't reckonin' on it being a sociable meeting at all if I catch up with him. In fact, Mr Clinton and his boys will be right put out if me and my pard get within pistol range of him. Laid out, if things go our way, ma'am, in the undertaker's parlour.'

'You'll need more than you're wearing now if you do meet up with Clinton,' Frenchy Belle said. 'Or it will be you and your pard that's laid out. Clinton ain't in town at present. Rode out to Jackson City, Missouri, so I heard. Three of his boys are still here though and he's got another four, five hardcases hangin' around somewhere so you ain't embarking on some picnic.'

Ira favoured Frenchy with a smug, cocky smile. 'The only place them boys you spoke of are hangin' around is Boot Hill, for keeps.' Then he told her of the fighting in the valley and how he and Will were determined to put paid to the trouble by killing Clinton or drawing the short straw themselves.

Frenchy Belle's mouth rounded in amazement. 'Well I'll be damned,' she said softly. 'And here's me thinking that you were just an innocent country boy on his first trip to town from the cabbage patch to sow his wild oats.' She got up from her chair and took the cup from Ira. 'Let me refill your cup, Ira, with a touch of something stronger, a glass of my special brandy. You've made my day already. Clinton's boys used to rough up my girls when the drunken bastards come in for their pleasures. Anyone that gives them a taste of what they're fond of dishing out is a lifelong friend of mine. And I'd break the house rules to favour him somewhat. That means any of my girls for free.' Frenchy Belle ass-shuffled to the edge of her chair, looking Ira directly in the eyes. 'Any girl he fancies, if you get my drift, Ira.'

Ira wasn't blind to the invitation in her look. He thought of her, jaybird naked, plump, soft and warm, sweet-smelling, and the hard, dangerous life devoid of the pleasures of women he'd lived for so long. Like, he thought, some warrior monk. Then he thought of Mr Harding watching out there in the street with the distinct possibility of three brush boys closing in on him with pistols in their hand and murder in their souls and his blood rapidly cooled.

Reluctantly he said, 'I'm sorely tempted, ma'am, sorely tempted to take up your invite to share your bed for a short spell. But me and my pard, as I told you, are here on dangerous business and I can't let him face it on his ownsome a minute more than it's absolutely necessary. He's out there on the street waiting for me right now.' He gave Frenchy Belle a sorrowful-faced grin. 'I'll just have to make do with the coffee and the brandy while you tell me anything else you know about Clinton and his gang.'

There were five public buildings in Will's line of sight from his seat on the front stoop of the general dealer's store. Two saloons, the town marshal's office, the church meeting hall and the cathouse. It seemed early in the day for the cathouse to be open for business and the marshal's office and the meeting hall weren't likely places where ex-Missouri brush boys would idle away their leisure time so Will hawk-eyed the two saloons.

It also must have been too early for the regular drinking men to be bellied up to the bars for Will only saw two men enter the far saloon and none at all go in the one nearest to him. But three men did come out of that saloon and walked along the boardwalks in his direction. As they neared him Will's face tensed up, wary-eyed and reaching behind him he drew out his pistol and laid it down across his knees, still gripping the butt. One of the men was the bastard that took part in the gunfight at Mr Brook's holding. He'd no doubts that the other two were the rest of the last of the Clinton gang.

Will looked along the street to the saloon but could see no sign of a weasel-faced man following them so he opined that Clinton had already left on his trip to Jackson City. He brought his gaze back on to the three marauders, still coming his way, and gently eased back the hammer of the Colt. What was occupying his mind most was whether he could hold them off till Mr Brooks came running up like old Stonewall's cavalry at the sound of gunfire in the street. Trying to see some edge in a dangerous, tricky situation, Will optimistically reasoned that once the marauders cleared the whorehouse they'd have the sons-of-bitches surrounded, that's if two men could surround three men.

Will saw the three stop outside the cathouse, exchange a few words that he couldn't hear, then two of them entered the building. The marauder that could finger him and Mr Brooks was the man left on the stoop. Will frantically wondered how the marauders had found out that at least one of the sodbusters from the valley was close on their trail and in the cathouse. Their tactics, two men going inside, one man blocking the way of escape, certainly smelled of them going in for a killing rather than just a social call.

He couldn't go and help Ira as long as the man who had seen him face to face was on the porch. That dumb-assed move could get him shot down before he'd got halfway across the street. That would be no goddamned help to Mr Brooks at all. Mr Brooks would have to do the holding out once the shooting started. When it did, Will reckoned that it would draw the man on the door's attention from the street, give him that few seconds of time to cross to the cathouse unseen.

Will got slowly to his feet, holding the Colt loosely down by his right leg, and leaned against the store front like a casual lounger, in the shadow of the porch roof. But ready to move as though his ass was on fire when the moment came.

'All I know about Mr Phil Clinton, Ira,'

Frenchy Belle said, 'is that he's a mean sonuvabitch that has a bunch of like-minded bastards riding with him all willing and happy to hurt folk for a price. But you know that already, don't you? M'be one of my girls has heard of who he visits in Jackson City. I'll ask them before you ride out. Now do...'

The sudden bursting open of the door and the appearance of two men with pistols in their hands in her private room stopped Frenchy Belle's talking in mid-flow. The two pistols swung in his direction as Ira slowly rose to his feet.

'Don't do anything foolish, mister, just put your hands up real high,' Vince snarled, 'and you won't get hurt none. We ain't lookin' for trouble, unless you make it for us.'

Ira did as he was told, tight-nerved, waiting to take advantage of any break that came his way. Whoever the pair of gunmen were they hadn't come for him or he would have been lying dead and bleeding on Frenchy Belle's fine rug. Frenchy Belle didn't take the invasion of her privacy so

150

calmly. She leapt up from the sofa, her fine bone china cup and saucer shattering to pieces as they hit the floor.

Red-faced and angry she yelled, 'What the hell do you two bums mean by bursting in here waving pistols at me and my guest? I'll have a word with Clinton about this!'

Ira somehow managed to control the natural impulse, knowing that the men were part of the Clinton gang, to grab for his pistol and start shooting, and to hell with the outcome. Then he remembered he was an ex-veteran blue belly, who had waited many a time before, guts all screwed up, for the charging reb line to get real close before loosing off a volley that would end their shooting and hollering. He gritted his teeth, biding his time. The assholes weren't close enough yet.

Vince grinned at Frenchy Belle. 'Me and Joe ain't workin' for Clinton any more. We've took up with workin' for ourselves. Our first job is to relieve you of your week's takin's we know you got stashed in some tin box hereabouts. So just stop your screechin' and get it out from where you've got it hidden then we can leave you and that fella there to do what he intends doin'.'

'I'll see the pair of you in hell first!' Frenchy Belle spat out.

Vince's face darkened. 'Now don't come on all tough with us, you old bitch. Cal's downstairs and he'd be eager to cut up your girls' pretty faces with that big Bowie he totes around with him. Think of how that would make your takin's drop, Frenchy. Not countin' the pain and grief it will cause the girls.'

'Do you gents mind if I lower my hands?' Ira said. 'While you are persuading the lady to hand over the cash?' Taking a chance he lowered his right hand and brushed his jacket open. 'See, I ain't carrying. I only came to bounce the madam here. You can burn the whole goddamned whorehouse down for me, I wouldn't give a shit.' He gave them a beaming country boy's vacant smile. And still waited, blood still pounding hard, to see if they would fall for his ploy. He was banking on them not wanting any shooting. Noise would alarm the lawman in Two Forks and have him come racing up the stairs to see what the hell was going on in the whorehouse.

Four beady, suspicious-glinting eyes slowly looked him up and down, seeing the absence of a pistol belted across his belly. 'OK, mister,' Vince said, 'but don't try any funny business or you're dead.'

Ira flashed them the hayseed's smile once more. 'Gents, I ain't come off mah pa's farm to this here town to go and get mahself shot. As I said I came here to get me a woman.' He gave Frenchy Belle a slight nod as he finished speaking.

Frenchy Belle gave Ira a puzzled glance sensing that he was sending her a message but she didn't know quite what the hell it was. She guessed though that she was to go along with the marauders' demands.

'OK, you bastards,' she said, 'I'll get you the cash box, but I'll get the marshal to raise up a posse to hunt you down.'

Vince grinned. 'You do that Frenchy but we'll be long gone before then.' His voice and face steeled over. 'Now do as you just said, get the box, as I told the hick there, no tricks. We don't want to hurt you but we will if you try to push your luck, savvy?'

Frenchy Belle gave them an extra venomous glare then walked across to the roll top desk in the far corner of the room. The marauders' gaze and their pistols had swung away from Ira to focus on Frenchy Belle. Ira gave an inner smile. Their greed was to be their downfall. Slowly he reached behind his back, Frenchy Belle's sliding back of the desk's top deadening the slight click as he eased back the Colt's hammer. The waiting game was over.

Ira fleetingly thought that m'be he could wing the pair of them so that they could be questioned about Phil Clinton. But violent living men with pistols drawn and cocked have to be dead or near to it before they ceased to be a danger. There was no sense in him getting shot this close to the end of the game. Besides, there was Frenchy Belle to consider. She could get herself wounded, or worse, by shells flying from wild shooting guns.

Taking a deep breath Ira yanked out his pistol, the foresight ripping his shirt as he pulled it free, and fanned off four loads in Gatling gun rapidity. The small fusillade caught the marauders in the act of turning to combat the unexpected threat. The fearful pain of the lower body hits folded them in the middle, gasping, hands dropping pistols, to clutch at their bellies in their dying agonies. The force of the shells twisted them back away from Ira to fall sideways to the floor in a clatter of broken and upturned furniture.

A horrified Frenchy Belle watched their life's blood seeping into her fine ankle-deep rugs and tried not to throw up. She felt her age and some. Anything but pretty. Ira, face fixed in a tight-mouthed grimace, walked over to them thumbing reloads into the

Colt. Temporarily deafened by his shots he didn't hear the sound of feet running along the hall, but he heard Frenchy Belle's scream of 'Look out Ira!'

He pulled Frenchy Belle down to the floor with him as the shells fired from Cal, poking his pistol round the edge of the door, and ripped into the bed behind which they were sheltering. Ira gave the scared Frenchy Belle, huddled tight against him, an it's-going-to-be-OK smile. He didn't think it was going to be OK at all. The bastard had them between a rock and a hard place. And he cursed himself for forgetting that there had been three marauders. A deadly lapse of memory that could get him killed.

Two shots sounded outside in the hall and Ira saw the man who had him pinned down come stumble-footing into view, aimlessly pumping shells into the ceiling. He brought his pistol up and cut loose at him as the marauder crumpled up at the knees and fell to the floor. He had fired at an already dead man.

'Are you OK, Mr Brooks?' Will called out, then stepped cautiously into the room, pistols in both hands.

'Yeah, it's all over, Mr Harding,' Ira replied. 'Thanks to you.' He stood up and helped Frenchy Belle on to her feet.

'I couldn't come in any sooner,' Will said. He pointed to the man he'd shot. 'That bastard was watching the entrance and he's the fella that knew us, Ira. As soon as the shootin' started he dashed upstairs to see what was going on, I followed him.' He touched his hat in greeting at Frenchy Belle. 'Please to meet you, ma'am. Though it ain't the most pleasant social occasion to make your acquaintance.'

Frenchy Belle, still clinging to Ira's arm, gave them both a trembling-lipped look. She'd seen some cool polite characters in her time but Mr Brooks and Mr Harding were the coolest, wildest sons-of-bitches she'd ever met. Her nerves had settled down somewhat for her to acknowledge Will's greeting with a wan smile. 'I don't know about you fast-shootin' gents but I need a drink. It isn't every day I get three dead men stretched out on my living-room floor messing up my rugs.' She walked out on to the hall and yelled, 'Bob, Jack! Get your asses up here, pronto and get this trash outa my room!'

Papers had been signed by Will and Ira, witnessed by Frenchy Belle that they had acted in self-defence in the preventing of an armed robbery, after which the marshal told them they were free to leave town. Frenchy Belle made Ira promise that if he passed through Two Forks again he was to call on her and m'be they could partake in something he hadn't time for this time round. Always providing he wasn't too occupied by the shooting down of thieving desperados in her room she added with a smile. This time when they rode out they openly wore their guns. There was no need for subterfuge any longer. They had the edge, a fair description of Phil Clinton, and he was ignorant of their looks, and unaware that he was being trailed.

Ira had picked up another piece of information concerning Clinton. Frenchy Belle, as she had promised, had asked her girls if they had heard any talk about Clinton's habits and haunts when not in Two Forks. She's been told by one of them that a member of the gang that was pleasuring her one time mentioned that Murphy's Bar was the gang's favourite watering-hole when they were in Jackson City, Missouri. That lead, thought Ira, could save them a lot of time. Jackson City was a big place to look for one man, even though they'd been told of his likeness. As Will told Ira, every other Missourian he'd met during the war was a weasel-faced hombre.

Frenchy Belle came out on her porch and as they rode out she waved and called out, 'Good luck! And take care!' Ira gave her a wave back.

Will grinned at him. 'You never did get to

mix pleasure with business, did you, Mr Brooks?'

'I never did,' Ira replied. 'The business was a lot more serious than I expected. Darned harrowin' in fact. Kinda knocked all suchlike pleasurable thoughts from my mind. I must be getting old, Mr Harding.'

Will thought of the widow Meg McDowell and the time he was spending hard-assing it across Kansas and now Missouri and what lay ahead of him could end his time for ever. Time that in different circumstances could have been spent with her. 'I hope we have the time to get a lot older, Mr Brooks,' he said bleakly.

TWELVE

Wilmore Newcombe felt like bursting into tears. His land-grabbing scheme was falling apart. Time was fast running out for him, or to be more precise, for that back-shooting son-of-bitch, Phil Clinton, to put it together again before the railroad surveyors came to the same conclusion he had months ago; that the valley was ideal for the new spur line.

He couldn't understand why Clinton had fallen down on the job of clearing the sodbusters out of the valley. He had thoroughly checked out the ex-guerilla leader. Men that looked and talked tough were a dime a dozen in Missouri but he'd discovered that Clinton was the genuine article. Wanted by both Reb and Unionist authorities for crimes that would have hung him and his band of grandmother-throatcutters several times over. 'Bloody' Bill Anderson was dead, William Quantrill badly wounded in a Union prison, so he had hired the best available man for the job.

He should have by now been sitting nice and comfortable on his ass waiting for the railroad lawyers to come knocking at his office door with fat cheques in their hands pleading with him to sell the valley to their bosses. Instead what had he got? Why, the weasel-faced bastard telling him that he'd failed to frighten the sodbusters out of the valley and that if he still wanted the land he'd have to shell out more cash for him to raise up another bunch of raiders. To make up for the men he'd lost in the valley. That got him thinking of what breed of men worked the land in the valley. Men that cut hard-men like the men Clinton ran down to size. Wilmore Newcombe stirred uneasily on his chair. Somebody, he felt, was striding across his grave.

Of course he had to agree to Clinton's

demands. It was sink or swim time for the Newcombe Land Development Company. He was playing in a poker game for big stakes. If he didn't win the whole god-damned pot he could be broke. So he just handed the money over to Clinton and tried not to look too concerned about it. He would have liked to have said that this time he hoped that he'd hear some news to his advantage for all the cash he'd put up front, till he saw the look in Clinton's eyes. He was well aware that Clinton was a hard, mean man, he'd hired him for that trait. Now he was hard, mean and mad, crazy as they came. 'Mr Newcombe,' he had said, 'you'll get your stinkin' valley, it's personal now. Though you might have to dig a lot of graves before you can show the land to the railroad people.' The smile Clinton gave him only confirmed that he was right. Clinton was crazy as a coot.

Phil Clinton rode at the head of eight men. Not as good or as disciplined as the old gang but he reckoned they were not squeamish about the shedding of blood. With Vince, Cal and Joe waiting for him in Two Forks, Tex at Plainsville, the boys would be up to full fighting strength. He gave a mad-assed grin. He had brought something else, a little extra firepower to throw at the sodbusters, a full case of blasting powder sticks. Enough to blow every damn sodbuster in the valley to Kingdom Come.

'I'm glad that plump little madam told us where Clinton's hangout is, Mr Brooks,' Will said as they dismounted outside Murphy's Bar. 'If we had to make a tour of all the gin palaces, gambling halls and cathouses in Jackson City we would be grey-bearded old-timers before we finished the rounds.'

They walked shoulder to shoulder into the bar, two walking tall, hard, bearded men. Trail dust grey shrouding their clothes. Pistols sheathed on right hips, another for all to see sticking above the waistbands of their pants, right hands holding rifles. Armed up like real prodding men. Although they had description of Clinton they couldn't pick out his likeness among the crowd of drinkers without going up to each table for a closer look. Such nosiness was a sure way of getting themselves into trouble without getting any nearer to Clinton.

'Look for a sonuvabitch with a tail and horns sproutin' out of his head, Mr Harding,' Ira side-mouthed. 'Clinton's earned them.'

Will laid the big Sharps on the bar and leaning across he buttonholed the nearest barkeep. 'I heard that a Mr Phil Clinton is hirin' hard-riding men,' he said. 'Is he still in town?' He hoped that his reasoning that Clinton had come to see his paymaster to press him for more cash to build the gang up again was right or the barkeep would think that he was talking through his hat.

The barkeep looked at Will and then at Ira and back again to Will. He had never seen such a stone-faced, frightening looking bastard since he'd first donned a barkeep's apron. The younger fella was running his old pard a close second. He smiled real good, the customer-always-has-the-edge grin. Especially one that totes a big rifle. Christ, the barkeep thought, one shot from that cannon and the saloon would be minus one side wall.

'Yeah, that's right, mister,' he said. 'Clinton was hirin' but he got all the men he wanted, rode out early this morning.'

'Are you sure?' asked Will, feeling a growing chill inside him knowing where Clinton and his new gang of bully boys were heading for. Then he cursed himself, for no good reason at all, just to ease some of the tension the disappointment at getting within grabbing distance of his quarry and missing him had built up.

'Sure I'm sure,' the barkeep said, not too protestingly in case it got the big man's dander up higher noting that what he'd told him had already upset him more than somewhat. 'I saw him leave town myself. He came out of Wilmore Newcombe's office, just across the street there, came in here and called his boys out. The next thing I saw was their horses kickin' up the dust as they rode out. M'be Mr Newcombe can tell you where Clinton's headin' for and you could catch up with him, ask him yourself if he's takin' any more boys on.'

Will glanced at Ira, the hunter's look back in his eyes again, then back to the barkeep. 'What line of business is this fella, Newcombe, in?'

'Why wheelin' and dealin' in land, mister,' the barkeep said. 'It's right there on his shingle, "The Newcombe Land Development Company". He buys up land he figures some big rancher or m'be the railroad wants then makes them pay through the nose to get it. Just moved into town from back east someplace.'

'Now we know "why", Mr Harding,' Ira said grimly. 'Let's go and pay the man a visit.'

The barkeep watched them leave the bar

with a feeling he'd unwittingly sicced a load of trouble on Mr Wilmore Newcombe. The pair didn't seem to be men that dealt in real estate unless it was in six feet plots in some Boot Hill. Walking across to Wilmore Newcombe's office Ira said, 'How the hell did we miss a bunch of riders on the trail, Mr Harding? We should have seen their trail-dust at least.'

'Mr Clinton thinks like an Injun,' Will said. 'He'll have led his men out of town in any direction but Kansas before he swung round and headed south-east. The sonuvabitch won't want anyone to know where he's makin' for. Prevents any lawmen from tyin' him in with the raids in the valley. What's troublin' me, Mr Brooks, is what we do when we confront Wilmore Newcombe. We ain't got enough evidence to convince any court of law to arrest him. And if we take the law in our hands we'll end up in jail.'

Mr Harding, Ira thought, had never shown himself to be a fretting man but though his face still looked as though it had been chiselled out of a lump of rock he could see the worry mirrored in his partner's eyes. The anxiety knowing that every minute wasted here in Jackson City. Clinton and his wild boys were getting that much closer to the valley and the widow McDowell.

'I know how you're feelin', Mr Harding,' he said. 'I feel the same, thinking of old Jake, the widow McDowell and the rest of the valley folk we ain't there to help when Clinton hits them again. But this fella, Newcombe, is the head of the snake. If we don't scotch him somehow he'll keep hiring more men to do his bidding even if we could ass-kick it back to the valley and put paid to Clinton once and for all. We'll just have to convince the land-grabbing bastard that staying in Jackson City won't be healthy for him but fast.' Ira gave a mirthless grin. 'Just hold back a spell, I'll go and get my hangin' rope. A good idea could work twice.'

Wilmore Newcombe glanced up in annoy-ance when his office door opened and two men came in without a by-your-leave knock on the door. As far as he was concerned Clinton had got all the money he was getting off him and if the two saddle-tramps standing in front of his desk had been sent by him to wheedle more cash out of him, or come to tell him that Clinton had hit another snag, they could go to hell. They could tell their boss that and he'd hire another bunch of Missourians to do the job.

Then suddenly it entered his mind that Clinton wouldn't send any of his men to see him, that had been arranged at the beginning of the deal, one to one meeting, so that the Newcombe Land Development Company wouldn't be seen to be involved with ex-Border Ruffians, lawbreakers. And furthermore he had seen Clinton ride out of Jackson City hours ago. When the elder of the two pushed the big rifle he was holding hard against his nose, jarring his head back with such force that it made his spine click painfully, he knew for certain that they were not Clinton's men. Pop-eyed at looking down his nose at the tip of the rifle barrel he somehow managed to gasp out, 'Wh ... who the hell are you ... and what do you want?'

'We're from Big Creek valley, across in Kansas,' Will grated. 'The place your hired bully boy, Clinton, and his gang are waging war against the homesteaders so that you pick up their land cheap and sell it to the railroad company dear.'

In a boldness he was far from feeling Wilmore Newcombe tried to bluff it out. 'I don't know what you're talking about, Clinton... Big Creek valley. I run a legitimate business here.'

Will pressed his head further back with the Sharps till Newcombe felt that his neck was going to snap. 'Mister, don't waste our time,' he said. 'We know Clinton came back to Jackson City to get himself some more boys to replace the ones we killed.' Will gave him a cold, you-better-believe-it smile, and Wilmore felt the acidity of bile at the back of his throat. 'One fella took a while in dying,' Will continued. 'Before he passed over he signed a piece of paper naming you as the man bankrolling the operation. Now if you were to cooperate by pulling up stakes and leave Jackson City I might not take it along to the marshal to let him deal with it.'

Wilmore Newcombe may have been a chicken-livered eastern dude but he knew all the ins and outs of the finer points of the law; sailed over the line often enough to have checked out every legal and illegal loophole that could be squeezed through. Managing a weak but confident grin he said, 'The marshal won't be able to make a case of it. You wouldn't be able to prove it, it would be my word against a dead outlaw's.'

'I told you that the bastard wouldn't listen to reason!' Ira snarled, face twisted in a savage mask. He pushed Will aside and grabbing hold of Wilmore yanked him out of his chair, clearing the cocky grin from his face. Before Wilmore had time to protest at his rough handling he felt the roughness of a rope being slipped over his head and pulled tight. He struggled wildly but the rope only sawed deeper into his neck. Just allowing him to breathe to stay alive, not enough for him to fill his lungs to give out a scream of pure piss-pants terror. He felt a knee dig sharply in the small of his back, propelling him remorsely towards the open balcony window and the drop into the street below, and the jerking neck-breaking sudden halt. Wilmore Newcombe made gurgling noises at the back of his throat and burst into tears.

'Let him go!' Will cried. 'It's murder you're doin' and I want no part in it!'

'Balls, murder,' said Ira, face still working in mad-anger, still pushing Wilmore towards the window. 'The men this sonuvabitch hired burnt my house down, ruined me. I'm only doin' the law's work a bit quicker that's all. If you ain't got the stomach to watch then get to hell outa it, but don't try to stop me!'

Will pointed the Sharps at Ira. 'If you don't ease off on that rope, cousin or not, I'll plug you for keeps.'

Mouthing obscenities Ira reluctantly let go of the rope and pushed Wilmore away from him. Wilmore fell to the floor and clutched Will tightly round the knees. 'I'll leave town!' he cried. 'Give me time to go to my hotel and pack that's all!' He cast a terrified look behind him at the crazy man with the rope. The crazy man was wondering how long he could have kept his wild hillbilly image up before Wilmore Newcombe cracked. A noose sure put the shits up a man, Ira thought.

'That's a promise?' said Will, giving Wilmore a kindly, fatherly look as he helped him on to his feet.

Wilmore couldn't trust himself to speak, making do with nodding his head vigorously.

'A wise decision, Mr Newcombe,' Will said. 'I take it you'll be on the next eastbound out from the depot?' He began straightening Wilmore's necktie and brushing down his jacket. Wilmore gave him the shake of the head again. 'There's two brothers of his,' Will said, pointing with his chin at the still glowering Ira. 'Madder than him, getting drunker by the minute in some saloon or other. If they find out I've let you go and I can't persuade them otherwise, there's more than a fifty-fifty chance that it will be me danglin' over the balcony with a rope round my neck. But I'm willing to take that chance rather than take part in a lynchin'.'

In a stumbling walk, nervously jerking his head round for a fear-filled-eyed look at Ira standing on the balcony, Wilmore, flanked by Will, made his unsteady way to his hotel.

Will met up with a wide-smiling Ira at the livery barn, both horses saddled up and ready to go for the long ride back to the valley.

'Any problems?' Ira asked.

Will shook his head. 'He practically held my hand like a little lost kid all the way to the depot. Saw him seated in a coach and gave him a real friendly wave as the train pulled out. I reckon that Mr Wilmore

Newcombe won't venture this side of the Mississippi ever again.' Po-faced he added, 'Mr Brooks, you should have been an actor, you almost had me pissing my pants.' As an afterthought he said, 'You were kiddin', you wouldn't have gone through with it, would you?'

'I don't rightly know, Mr Harding,' Ira said, equally serious-faced. 'At one time I was frightening myself. I was getting the same feelings I had in some clearing in the Wilderness battles when you reb bastards were coming down hard on us blue bellies, red-eyed mad feelings.'

'We were all a little touched in the head those days, Mr Brooks,' Will replied. 'Or we couldn't have survived. And we've got to stay that way if we want to get the better of that bunch ahead of us. They'll not fall for any bluff that's for sure. Killing them is the only way to stop them.'

Thinking on that sobering statement kept the pair of them silent for a long time on the trail.

THIRTEEN

Frenchy Belle drew back from the window, partly hiding behind the drapes, as the nine riders passed below her balcony. Border scum, prodding men, Phil Clinton's men. Men that were riding to that valley in Kansas that Mr Brooks had told her about to carry on with the killing and burning. Clinton would know by now about the fate of the three men he'd left in Two Forks and where they'd met it. Clinton would be mad enough, if she showed herself, to start shooting her place up to get even.

More disturbing to Frenchy Belle's peace of mind was that Clinton's presence in town meant that Mr Brooks and Mr Harding had failed in their mission to put paid to Clinton. Clinton alive could mean that they were dead. The way she had read them it had been a kill or be killed trail they were following. Frenchy Belle's emotions and feelings were only as deep as the professional whore's smile yet for some reason or other she had more than a skin-deep feeling for Ira Brooks. Would have been delighted to have him share her bed with her for a session, at no charge at all.

Frenchy Belle smiled, breaking the goddamned rules of the house. But what the hell she thought, rules are meant to be broken once in a while. Mr Brooks and Mr Harding were a special breed of men, not coming her way often. Men willing to put their lives on the line so that other patch-assed levi sodbusters could work their strip of dirt land in peace. Why is it, Frenchy Belle said to herself as she watched the marauders' trail-dust drifting away, that the good always seemed to get the shit end of the stick and bastards like Clinton come out on top? What the hell, she thought, and sniffing back her tears went across to her dressing table to fix up her face ready for the start of the day's business.

Frenchy Belle needn't have worried about Phil wanting to shoot up her place, he had other things on his mind. He was naturally put out that he was now three men short but they were dead and gone and that was that. Crying wouldn't bring them back. What was tinging his angry, wound up tightness feeling was a feeling he'd never had before; fear. The sodbusters weren't just killing his boys in the valley, two of them were seeking him out, killing his boys as they were closing in on him. Leaving their own ground and bringing the fight to him. And they were men, Phil reluctantly conceded, who knew what they were about.

Phil also reckoned he knew who the sons-of-bitches were. The fella with the big Sharps, and the dynamite thrower. He gave a thin-lipped smile. This time he'd the dynamite. That pleasant thought eased some of his fear, though not enough to prevent him from looking along his back-trail for the distant shapes of two riders hellbent on killing him.

Frenchy Belle and her girls were sitting on the front porch of the whorehouse catching the cool early evening breeze before the hectic night trade got into full swing. 'Ain't them the two fellas that did all that shootin' in your room, Miss Frenchy?' one of the girls said.

Frenchy Belle got up from the swing-seat and stepped to the edge of the porch. 'Well I'll be damned,' she breathed. 'It sure is. And here's me thinking that they were dead.' She wanted to laugh and cry at the same time. If she'd been on her own she would have unashamedly let her feelings of relief come to the surface by blubbering like a young girl. But she didn't want her girls to think that old Ma Belle, the name she knew they called her behind her back, had gone soft in her middle-age.

Ira and Will drew their horses up alongside the porch, Ira giving Frenchy Belle a weary-assed grin as he leaned back in his saddle.

'You asked us to pay you a call the next time we hit Two Forks but like the last time we're only passing through, hurriedly like.'

'The reason for your haste, Mr Brooks,' said Frenchy Belle, 'passed through here six, seven hours back. Nine reasons, counting Phil Clinton. So I reckon you didn't stop him after all.'

'No, we didn't, ma'am.' It was Will that answered her. 'Never saw the sonuvabitch. It wasn't a wasted journey though. Mr Brooks gave the man who pays Clinton's wages to do the raidin' such a scare that he won't be visiting these parts again. There's only Clinton and the team he's managed to rake together now.'

Frenchy Belle ran a critical eye over Ira and Will, and saw the tired, tension-lined unshaven faces. 'You ain't likely to stop them, Mr Harding. It's nine men you're after. The state the pair of you are in you wouldn't last another couple of hours before you fell off your horses with exhaustion. That's if your horses ain't dropped dead

181

before that.'

'We aim to feed and water them before we start off along the trail again,' Ira said, testily.

Frenchy Belle snorted derisively. 'Those horses need resting, the same as you do.' Close-eyeing them she said, 'There must be someone in that valley of yours real special to one of you for you to want to go and kill yourselves. Because that's more than likely what you'll be doing taking on nine desperados the state you're both in. I know that you're handy men with pistols, but you ain't that good, no offence meant, gentlemen.'

'No offence taken, ma'am,' Will said. 'But that's the way it has to be. We can't let Clinton get a bigger lead on us than he's already got.'

Ira was conscious of what was driving Will on. He was also aware of the extra risks they were taking. Pushing their luck, if they were due any, to the limit and beyond. Frenchy Belle was right. Looking at it realistically they hadn't much chance of getting the better of Clinton and his gang. Going up against them deadbeat wouldn't help the widow McDowell or anyone else in the valley. And as sure as hell it wouldn't help them any other than help them to get a hole in Boot Hill damn quick.

'The lady speaks sense, Mr Harding,' Ira said. 'We need to lie up for a few hours, the horses are all in. It gives them the chance for a good feed and a rest. And we're pushing ourselves too hard.'

Will sat for a moment or two, silent, face unreadable, then he sagged loosely in his saddle. 'Yeah, you're right, Mr Brooks.' He tired-smiled Frenchy Belle. 'It is someone special that's got me not thinkin' straight. We'll see to our horses then find a place to have three, four hours sleep.'

'Ain't no need, Mr Harding,' Frenchy Belle said. 'I'll see to it that the horses are attended to. And you can use one of my spare rooms to rest up in. Velda, show these gentlemen to the back room.'

Ira grinned at Will. 'You heard the boss lady, Mr Harding.'

'We'll take up your offer, ma'am,' Will said and swung down off his mount. 'For three hours.'

Frenchy Belle waited till Velda had led Ira and Will indoors then giving the other girls on the porch a sweeping, warning look said, 'You girls let them sleep, understand? I want none of you sneakin' upstairs to try and earn yourselves a few extra dollars. Now one of you go and get hold of Jack and tell him I want him, here out front.'

Frenchy Belle told her bouncer to take the horses to the livery barn to be fed and watered. Then to hire four fresh horses from Tate, two of them to be saddled up, the other two to be used as packhorses, carrying enough rations and water for two men and the horses to last three days.

'And don't let that horse thief palm four pieces of crow bait on to you, Jack,' Frenchy Belle said. 'I want the best horse flesh he's got or tell him that I'll let his wife know the antics he gets up to in here on a Friday night, the night he's supposedly working late.'

It seemed to Ira that his head had just touched the pillow when he felt himself being shaken awake by Will. It was still dark, a longways from dawn.

'One of the girls has knocked on the door,' Will said. 'Says there's a hot breakfast ready downstairs for us.'

'Did you sleep OK?' Ira asked. 'I think I died for a few hours.'

'So-so,' replied Will. Images of the widow McDowell's shack going up in flames prevented him from having no more than a few minutes fitful dozing at a stretch. Her screams as she watched her home burning rang most undreamlike in his ears.

'These horses are only a loan, Mr Brooks,' Frenchy Belle said. 'When you bring them back you can pick up your own mounts.' She nearly said if you're alive to bring them back, but she didn't want to put an Indian curse on Mr Brooks or his hard-faced pard. They were riding headlong into enough trouble as it was. Ira and Will had eaten well and felt fortified and rested, ready as they could ever be for whatever lay ahead of them. They'd been told by one of the girls as they were finishing their breakfast that their horses were out front and ready for them to ride out. She didn't tell that there were four horses or about the rations. Before they could thank her for her generous, un-expected offer, Frenchy Belle raised a hand.

'Don't thank me, boys,' she said. 'I'm beholden to you both. You saved me from being robbed and I always pay favours back. And as I said you've only got them on loan. Now get yourselves on the trail of that asshole, Phil Clinton. Mr Harding's been raring to go for the last hour or so and good huntin' to the pair of you.'

Will smiled. 'Now we're beholden to you, ma'am.' He touched his hat in a farewell gesture as he mounted his horse.

Ira was more open in his appreciation. Grinning broadly he pulled Frenchy Belle close and bending low, kissed her full and long on the mouth, conscious of the giggles of Frenchy Belle's girls behind him.

Red-faced and embarrassed as a young girl, Frenchy Belle pushed him away from her. 'Get the hell off my porch, you horn dog!' she growled in mock anger. 'Though the next time you come ridin' up this pike I hope that you'll stay a mite longer. These fleeting visits of yours ain't no good at all to either of us.'

She watched them ride off then turning to her girls, grave-faced, she said, 'I know you, Conchita and you Velda, still go to mass and as I ain't a prayin' woman, and it would be right hypocritical for me to turn into one now, I'd be obliged if you could say a prayer, or light a candle or whatever, the next time you go to church, for those two gentlemen. They're lookin' in on the Devil and they'll need God's help to see them through.'

FOURTEEN

Jake Mills cast a jaundice-eyed glance at his small command; Ma, Ben, Mr Levins and his boy Pat, and the widow woman, Mrs McDowell. The men crouching, boys became men in these circumstances, behind rifles poking through the firing slits of boarded-up windows. The two women were sheltering under a table, acting as reloaders, yet willing and capable to take the place of a rifleman if the need arose. Why, Jake thought, just to cheer himself up a little, he'd held off many an Indian warband with a lot less firepower. But this time it wasn't bare-assed hostiles who would quit and haul off and raid some other homestead if the fight wasn't swinging their way. The Missouri raiders were back, with a vengeance, dynamiting their way down the valley, intending to make an end of it. A no-quarter given fight. Jake was glad that he'd seen the widow McDowell's kids had left in the buggy to the safety of a neighbour's holding. He'd three less lives to worry about.

Jake had made some quick, hard decisions, had them thrust on him so to speak, in the last couple of hours. He only hoped they'd been the right ones or no one in this shack would be able to make another one – the raiders would see to that. Jake let out a growl of anger and shifting the plug of chaw in his mouth, he puckered up his lips to spit in his own special pail that Ma put out for him when he remembered he was in the widow McDowell's shack.

The day had started normally. Ben and Pat were out on their daily checking on Ira's and Will Hardin's homesteads, Jake hoping that the pair of them had caught up with the renegade boss and what was left of his gang and killed them all. Then he might get rid of the crick in his neck with looking up at the high ridge, praying to God he wouldn't see a line of horsemen along it. Ben and Pat hightailing it up to the shack brought him the shouted news that he'd been dreading to hear.

Ira, having no stock on his land, Ben and Pat only had to check that the shutters and doors on his shack and the locks on the outbuildings were secure against any stray wolf or coyote foraging around for food before moving on to Will Harding's property. They saw the riders from the rise as they were about to drop down into the shallow valley that Mr Harding's holding nestled in. Eight to ten of them as close as they could reckon at this distance milling around the shack. Then suddenly before their very eyes the shack blew apart, hurtling skywards, sideways, everyways, then came the bang. After the bang they heard the lighter cracks of rifle fire.

Two blood-drained faced boys looked at

each other. The night battle they'd taken part in had been exciting, blood stirring, for boys in their first gunfight. The odds had been in their favour; experts with guns, Mr Brooks and Mr Harding, standing alongside them. Now they realized that a gunfight isn't exciting at all when you're heavily outnumbered, just bowel-loosening frightening. Ben was halfway to his pa's holding, Pat lashing his horse alongside him, before the dust cloud raised by the dynamiting of the shack finally settled.

Ben and Pat pulled up their mounts in a haunch-sliding stop. Ben leapt off his horse and ran yelling into the shack, 'The sonsuvbitches are back, Pa! They've dynamited Mr Harding's shack, blew it all to hell! And they're killin' his stock!'

Normally Jake didn't allow his son to use strong language in front of him, especially in the shack when his ma was in earshot but he could see that Ben was all worked up and real scared. 'Calm down, son,' he said.

'How many son ... how many are there of them?'

'About nine or ten, I think, Pa,' Ben replied. 'Is that how many you reckon, Pat?'

Pat, who had followed Ben into the shack, said, 'That's about the tally, Mr Mills.' He gave Ben a nervous grin. 'We didn't hang round long enough to count them exact.'

'You did right,' Jake told them. 'Warning me was more important than staying and exchanging lead with them. You'd have only got yourselves killed.'

'What are we goin' to do, Pa?' Ben asked. 'They'll be comin' here after they pay a visit to Mr Brooks' place.'

'Quiet, boy,' Jake growled. 'I'm thinkin'.' Jake thought quickly and came up with a momentous decision just as quickly. The only one he could make, the way he read the situation. Ben was right. The marauders would come sweeping down the valley, Ira's shack being next on Clinton's list for destruction, then here, then on to the widow McDowell's holding. He walked out on to

192

the porch and gazed up at the neck-cricking ridge. A blasting stick thrown from there would land plumb down his shack's smoke stack. It would become a graveyard if he tried to hold out in it. A blown to bits shack can be rebuilt. Blown up folk have the habit of staying dead.

Now, if he recollected rightly, the widow's shack had cleared ground all round it. There was a chance there to keep the raiders at bay, in the daylight at least. Before darkness came he hoped that some of the nearby homesteaders would have rallied round in support at the widow's shack, make it their battleground. If they didn't he was only putting back his, Ma's, Ben's, Mrs Mc-Dowell's, Joe and his pa, if they joined him, chances of getting blown to bits by a few hours. Jake walked back indoors and began to give out his orders.

'Pat, you go back home,' he said. 'Tell your pa what you've seen. Tell him that I'm pulling out of here and making my stand at the widow McDowell's place. It'll be harder there for the raiders to get in real close to be able to throw their dynamite to harm us real badly. I'd rightly appreciate it if you and your pa will hold the shack with me. One thing more, Pat, and it's durn important, somehow we'll have to warn the rest of the homesteaders what's goin' on because we need as many guns as we can muster, we've got a real war on our hands, boy. Your pa can m'be work something out, OK?'

Pat nodded his head. 'OK, Mr Mills. Me and pa will meet up with you at Mrs McDowell's that's for sure.' He grinned at Jake. 'Even if I've got to strap him across his horse and lead him there.' Pat's face twisted in thought for a moment or two. 'M'be Ma could get the buggy out and do the warning. But don't worry we'll get the message passed on.'

'Good,' said Jake. 'Right, off you go then there's still things to do here.'

Once he'd seen Pat ride off Jake told Ben to hitch the bay to the wagon and let the stock loose and drive them well clear of the shack. He calculated that ten minutes would make no difference either way to the forthcoming battle and he owed Ma something for asking her to leave the home she had built up over the last twenty years, had the kids and raised them in it. While Ben was hurrahing the few head of cattle and hogs he owned with yells and pistol shots he gave Ma a hand to hide some of her special pieces of furniture in the gully behind the shack.

'We've still got more than when we first came here, Ma,' he said, trying to comfort her. 'Just to get even with the sonsuvbitches I'll let you have first shot at Clinton if we can spot him.'

Clinton had got some pleasure in blowing up the two shacks but he hadn't seen blood yet and sodbusters' blood, gallons of it, was the only thing that would put things right with him, give him the feeling that he was in control of the situation again. Moving south along the valley the next homestead to get a taste of Missouri brush boys evening up of the score would be the shack below the ridge where Tex had been winged.

Clinton waited on the ridge till the men who had gone down to the wrecked shack to finish off any sodbuster that was still showing signs of wanting to fight. When they returned they reported the same findings as at the other two shacks, not a sodbuster or any of his brood, not even the homestead's hound dog were alive or dead among the ruins. That worried Clinton. Set the fears he'd had since hearing of the killings of his boys at Two Forks nagging away at his insides again. It was turning out too easy for him. For sodbusters that had trailed him all the way to Two Forks, m'be even as far as Jackson City, then gun down three men, made Tex cut and run somewhere, it smelt wrong them giving up without a fight.

He opined that the first two shacks had been occupied by the sons-of-bitches that had done the hunting down of his boys but it puzzled him why this shack should be deserted. He knew from his previous raids into the valley it had been occupied by a family, an old man, his wife and a boy. They couldn't be coming along his back trail wanting to gun him down. M'be he was worrying too much, they could have pulled up stakes and lit out. The next shack to be presented with a couple of sticks of dynamite would be the widow's place. She could be long gone but that made no difference he would still close on her shack cautiously, real Indianlike. As much as he wanted to see blood Clinton had been tricked once and couldn't afford to lose this gang by being suckered again. The sod-busters must be waiting for him some-where.

Jake looked out of the shack window and saw everything as it should be. He glanced around the room to see if everyone was at their posts then peeked over the window ledge again and saw the marauders flitting through the brush and tree section on the far edge of the holding like grey shadows. Jake levered a shell into the firing chamber of his Winchester and mindful of the women and boys in the room he suppressed his strong desire to curse long and obscenely. Instead, in a calm, matter-of-fact voice, so as not to alarm the widow and Ma, he said, 'The marauders are here, this side, nine of the varmints. You'd better take over from me, Hank, you're the best shot in the cabin. Even better than Ma with her new store glasses on.' He grinned just to show how unconcerned he was, a lying grin. 'They're comin' in a mite cagey for hell-raising brush boys. I reckon the empty shacks they've come across has got them puzzled. One man will be comin' in close with the dynamite, Hank. Down him for keeps before he reaches that line of tree stumps or we won't be able to give them a fight. You boys keep the rest of the sonsuv ... gang's heads low. Just to let them know that it ain't goin' to be a walkover for them.'

Hank brought his rifle up and sighted on a

lone man, bent low, running in a zigzag track towards the shack, a thin shower of red sparks flowing from his right hand. He brought the rifle sights slightly ahead of the running figure then squeezed the trigger. All in the shack heard a thin scream as the marauder tumbled head-over-heels as though he had tripped over a tree stump causing the stick of dynamite to fly out of his outstretched hand. The man tried to regain his feet, seemed to find it too much hard work, and slipped back on to his face again. Then the dynamite exploded, lifting and blowing him away like a rag doll. The blast close enough to the shack to shatter the front windows and shower the porch with lumps of soil and stones.

One more raider was shot down by gunfire from the shack before they hurriedly went to ground. Jake let out a whoop of delight.

'First blood to us folks,' he said. 'Aim true, especially you, Hank, and we'll pull through OK.' Out of the side of his mouth he whispered to Hank, 'I hope your good lady wife has managed to raise us up some help for come dark those sonsuvbitches out there will have all the edge.'

Clinton knew he had the edge. Although he'd lost two men, the sodbusters, four rifles he counted, were making a stand. He wasn't being led deeper into the valley into some sort of a trap. As soon as night came he would be able to walk right up to the shack and place a couple of sticks of dynamite right outside the front door without the danger of stopping a lump of lead.

Will's face lengthened, grew gaunter, when he saw his shattered home, slaughtered stock, his life's work destroyed. By changing horses at regular intervals, army style, they had made up a lot of time on Clinton. The ruins of his shack were still smouldering so they were not far behind him. Will fervently prayed that they were close enough to the marauders for him not to be witnessing the same scene of destruction at Meg McDowell's holding. Silent-voiced they rode on to Ira's homestead.

Ira's response at seeing the broken, burnt timbers that had been his birthplace, the home where he had grown up, was to give a mirthless, cold-eyed grin. 'I seemed to be fated not to be able to spend any length of time in my home, Mr Harding,' he said. 'But I tell you this, Mr Clinton is sure fated not to spend much more time on this sweet earth doin' what he's doin' as long as I can climb on to a horse and wield a gun, for I'll kill him for sure. And that's a goddamned fact, neighbour!'

Before they made Jake Mills' holding, three fast riding horsemen caused them to reach for their rifles. As the riders drew nearer Ira pushed back his rifle into its boot.

'It's OK, they're valley folk, Mr Harding,' he said. 'The one on the black used to buy hogs off my pa.'

The riders brought Will and Ira up to date on what was happening in the valley. Of how Hank Levins' wife had come fireballing down the valley trail in her buggy hollerin' that the Missouri sons-of-bitches were dynamiting the homesteads. That old Jake Mills was forted up at the widow McDowell's place with her man and her boy to try and hold them back and wanted any man that could use a gun to come and help out.

'There's another five of us back along the trail a piece,' the homesteader said. 'Only the wagon they're comin' in lost a durn wheel. Take a while before they can fix it so us three who had horses come on ahead.'

Will felt some of the pressure he was feeling ease off a little and silently blessed Jake Mills for having the foresight to choose the more open ground at Meg's homestead to make a stand. It had taken a lot of guts for him to leave his shack, no doubt, Will opined, gone the same way as his and Mr Brooks'. He made a solemn promise there and then that he'd help old Jake to rebuild his shack before he started on his own.

Ira grim-faced Will. 'I sure hope they haven't downed them all, Mr Harding. I've got myself worked up into a real killin' mood.'

'Well let's go and see,' replied Will. 'I reckon Jake will be pleased to see us ride in,' and he dug his heels sharply into his horse's ribs that sent it into a back heel raising dust gallop. Ira and the other homesteaders following just as fast in his wake.

Will held up his hand and the small cavalcade came to a halt just below the lip of a slight downward slope that led to the McDowell holding.

'Wait here,' he said. 'I'll go on on foot and have a look at the lie of the land. There's twice as many of them as there are of us, mean, sonsuvbitches. No good giving them any more edge than they've already got by goin' in mad-assed without some sort of a plan.'

When Will looked over the crest at the homestead there was only desultory rifle fire coming from the shack and the raiders, bedded down in a depression in the ground, forming a tight half-circle around the right-hand side of the shack. Two more of them were firing at the shack from the left flank. Nightfall wasn't far away and he and Ira and the three much needed reinforcements would have to play their part in the action fast, before Clinton stepped up the tempo. He would only be waiting till dark then he and his cutthroats would close in on the shack, finishing off those that the dynamite hadn't already killed.

Will saw that the ground at the rear of the marauders' line was as flat and unbroken as the stretch of land in front of them. A man, he opined, could ride real fast along there, his horse's reins gripped between his teeth, aiming and firing two pistols with a fair degree of accuracy at the besiegers. Hitting some of them, scaring the pants off the rest. Flushing them out of the ditch into the gun sights of the rifles in the shack.

Of course the man he was thinking of doing the ass-kicking of his horse, blazing away with the pistols, would have to be an ex-reb. One that had been well versed in suchlike glory boy tactics by having soldiered with General Thomas J 'Stonewall' Jackson's hard riding brigade during the war, like himself. Will got to his feet and gave a hard-faced, the-die-is-cast-grin thinking that Mr Brooks seemed mad enough at Clinton to go down there with him to give the marauders a taste of hell.

He explained his plan to the others when he rejoined them and it was as he had thought, Mr Brooks was willing to ride with him. The three homesteaders were also keen to take part but as Will pointed out to them they were only armed with rifles, awkward to fire with good effect from the backs of fast-moving horses and hadn't the fire-power of two six-shot pistols. Besides, he told them, he would like them to go down and take on the marauders from the other side of the shack to draw their attention from the unpleasant surprise he had in store for them. Their firing would also let Jake and the rest of them in the shack know that they were no longer on their own.

The three homesteaders had left on foot to take up their firing positions. Ira and Will, after checking the actions and loads of their pistols, then mounted up and waited, blood racing. Eyes glazing over in taut-skinned-faces, minds blank of any other thought but the killings they were about to embark on.

They heard the three rifles open fire, the signal for the killing-time to begin. They rode away from the homestead for a few hundred yards before swinging round in the shack's direction again. Stopping on the edge of the brush and timberlined piece of land they took one final look at the line of men they were about to attack. They were all pouring lead at the shack and at the homesteaders' positions beyond it. So far so good, Ira thought, then out loud he said, 'Let's ride, Mr Harding.' He put his reins in his mouth, gripping them tight, thumbed back the hammers of the Colts, then weighed them lightly in his hands. He brought his feet up high and outwards from his horse before dropping them real hard into its flanks. Will saying, 'One more thing to do, Mr Brooks,' stayed their downward swing. 'Just to let Jake know in which direction we're comin' in from. Then he'll watch where he's firing.'

Will cupped his hands to his mouth and Ira heard the bubbling cry of the reb yell. He'd heard it scores of times, coming from hundreds of throats, always scaring the shit out of him. This close, although from a single voice, a man he was about to walk the line with, it still set his blood curdling and lifted the short hairs on the nape of his neck.

When the three rifles began their firing, Clinton didn't let them upset him. A dynamite stick would soon silence them. The more sodbusters he killed here the less there were to kill later on. The reb yell and the two riders thundering towards him and his boys, pistols firing like crazy did more than upset him. The uneasiness he'd felt on the trail from Two Forks had been justified.

When a man sees what his guts tells him is his fate closing in on him he is entitled to be scared.

All his adult life, with the help of his gang, he'd been the man that had done the frightening, killing, if he couldn't scare people into giving him what he wanted. Now these two hell-raisers were giving him the same treatment. Men, he'd acknowledged, who knew their business, and then some. Face twisting in a fear-based grimace, Clinton ate dirt and played dead as the Colt shells kicked up the dust alongside him till they rode by him.

The gang, bar-room bums, rounded up by Clinton in the saloons and gin palaces of Jackson City, were only with him for the cash he'd promised them with the added guarantee that they would have no trouble at all in the earning of it. Like money from home he had told them. Suddenly big trouble was hitting them, getting dead trouble, and they broke and ran for their horses. Three never made it out of the ditch.

Ira and Will's fast-shooting, flesh-tearing Colt shells hammered into their backs, finishing for ever their hopes of easy money times. Two more fell, downed in mid-flight by rifle fire from the shack. The only man left called it a day by stopping his running, throwing down his rifle, and raising his hands high with a yelled, 'I'm quitting! Don't shoot!' In no time at all Phil Clinton's second gang had gone the same bloody way as his first had.

Ira and Will drew up their horses, gulping the air as though they and not their mounts had been doing the running, to ride slowly back along the ditch to check on the bodies lying there, especially a mean, weasel-faced one. They left Jake and Hank, who had come bursting out of the shack, to round-up the only survivor of the small massacre. Their grins at each other at pulling a mad-assed stunt off and still being alive afterwards were as wild as the ride had been.

Clinton seized his chance. He could have backshot one, m'be both of them, but the sodbusters from the shack would gun him down. It was no good getting even then getting dead before he'd fully savoured his revenge. His face still pressed into the dirt, Clinton reached into his coat pocket and drew out a stick of dynamite and a match. He struck the match on his belt buckle and lit the fuse, then raising himself slightly he threw the stick at Ira and Will as they were swinging their horses around. Not wanting to move around too much in case he was spotted as being still alive, restricted his length of throw.

The dynamite fell well short and out of line to cause fatal or serious injuries to Ira and Will but the bang as it exploded sent the horses rearing, front-leg kicking, high in the air, unseating both of them. Jake and Hank spun round and fired at the running, bobbing figure they could only partly see through the dust spout raised by the explosion.

Ira got shakily to his feet. He had fallen heavily, unprepared, hadn't been able to brace himself before hitting the ground. He flexed his limbs and felt a stab of pain in his right leg, otherwise as far as he could tell no bones were broken. Will, a heavier built man, was not so fortunate. He had fallen real hard, awkwardly. Face twisted in pain, he struggled upright, holding his left shoulder.

'I think that I've busted my shoulder,' he groaned. 'I reckon that was a goin' away present from Mr Clinton,' he added.

'A few more yards closer, Mr Harding,' Ira said, still shaky-nerved. 'And we would have been away. On the road to the Pearly Gates. You go over to the shack and get that shoulder fixed. I'll see to the horses and things out here.'

The inside of the widow McDowell's shack had lost its look of an armed frontier outpost and was back to its normal domestic usage. The wagonload of reinforcements had arrived, in time to load the wagon with the dead marauders, (to see them decently buried), and the one prisoner. Jake and his family had left to spend the night with Hank at his shack, Billy promising to bring Mrs McDowell's children back home in the morning.

Will sat in front of the fire, his shoulder strapped up, face drawn and pale with pain. Ira sat at the table cleaning and oiling the four pistols, half-smiling at the sight of the hard-nosed Mr Will Harding being fussed over by the widow McDowell.

Will glanced across at Ira. 'You're aimin' to go after him, Mr Brooks, ain't you?'

'Yeah, I am,' Ira replied. 'It seems the thing to do, Mr Harding.'

'But why?' Mrs McDowell asked as she came in from the kitchen. 'His gang's all finished and the man that paid him to do the raiding, you told me, has left the territory. Clinton can be no danger to us now, surely?'

'Mr Brooks is right in his thinkin', Meg,' Will said. 'Clinton ain't a forgivin' man. We've made him eat crow, twice, and he won't have liked that at all. He'll come sneakin' back someday, when me or Mr Brooks are working on our land, riding along the trail, and he'll gun us down.' He looked back again at Ira. 'If you can wait a few days till my shoulder sets I'll ride with you.'

'There's no need, Mr Harding,' Ira replied. 'I'm only after one man, shouldn't cause me any problems I reckon, and I don't want the trail to get cold. You've got plenty to do here when you can use that arm, without wasting your time trailin' Clinton. All I've got is a pile of charred timbers to hold me back.'

'Well, if you say so, Mr Brooks,' Will said, reluctantly. 'But if you want any help at any time on the trail you let me know somehow and I'll be out as fast as I can make it.'

Ira saw the look of relief soften the worry lines on the widow McDowell's face at Will's decision. 'I do say so,' he said. He grinned. 'I'm not only trailin' Clinton, Frenchy Belle wants her horses back, remember?'

Meg McDowell wanted to ask who was

Frenchy Belle but she didn't like to poke her nose into men's business. Will Harding wasn't her husband yet.

Ira got up from the table and picking up his own pistols said, 'I'll go and see that the horses are bedded down OK. Then I'll get myself some shuteye. I want to be riding out at first light.' There was another reason for making his excuses, he didn't want to seem to be intruding between a man and his future wife. That was the way he opined things were shaping up between the widow McDowell and Mr Harding. If the hard-faced old reb got up enough courage to ask her to marry him.

'I'll have a hot meal ready for you before you ride off, and rations for the journey, Mr Brooks,' Mrs McDowell said. 'And thanks for all that you've done for me and my family.' She favoured Ira with a wan smile. 'It can't have been a very pleasant home-coming for you, all the killing and your home burnt down and all.'

'It sure wasn't ma'am,' Ira said. 'But it can

only get better.' Under his breath as he left the room he added, 'But not before Clinton is planted.'

FIFTEEN

Phil Clinton stood at the bar of the Palace saloon in Two Forks, the whisky in his glass hardly touched. A sunken-eyed, expressionless face stared back at him from the big mirror above the bar. A face of an already dead man? Clinton, not a superstitious man, shivered. He took a quick nervous pull at his whisky to calm himself down.

He'd seen the two sons-of-bitches fall off their horses when the dynamite had exploded but he'd been too busy dodging lead to see if they had been hurt real bad. He reckoned they could have been, though he couldn't believe that enough to put his life on the certainty that he'd put them out of action. Better to think that right now they could be pounding along the trail to Two Forks to see him laid out dead like the rest of his boys and get good and ready to meet them.

He could have pushed on to Jackson City, stretching the distance between him and his trackers, but that would be only putting off the day of reckoning. Till they were dead he had no future. Clinton's death-mask of a face snarled back at him from the mirror. Alive or dead he had no future. The Big Creek valley caper was definitely finished. All his dead men proved that. Even if Wilmore Newcombe was willing to part with more cash he wouldn't be able to hire men who knew it could be signing their own death warrants. Here in Two Forks was the place where things had to be settled by killing the bastards who would be searching the bars for him. Then he could consider his future options on how he was to earn his keep.

He had still the slight edge to do that. The sodbusters would reckon that he was on his own. The death's-head smiled at him. He wasn't. He'd made plans. In no way was he going to face his hunters on his own. Clinton didn't believe in all that hogwash about how a man should walk along Main Street to face his opponent man to man in a pistol shootout. All regular and above board. Indian-style of killing was the best, sneaky, by the bullet, the knife, beating their heads in with a rock. Anything that left him walking away from the action. He'd made arrangements for him to be able to do that.

'There's two hombres, big men, comin' along my back trail, the Plainsville trail,' he had told the old whisky soak that fetched and carried for the livery barn owner. 'You'll be able to pick 'em out, they'll have the look of men that's done a lot of hard-riding. You let me know, quiet-like, as soon as they hit town. I'll be along at the Palace, if I ain't there leave a message with one of the barkeeps. My name is Clinton, Phil Clinton. There'll be a bottle of redeye in it for you.'

As extra insurance Clinton had call on two men who fancied themselves as up and coming shootists to back him up in any forthcoming gunplay the sodbusters pushed him into making. Making the odds he reckoned three to two in his favour. He poured himself out another shot of the whisky. The face in the mirror began to come alive again, back to its normal snake-eyed meanness.

Frenchy Belle had seen Clinton come into town and by the expression she saw on his face he wasn't heading to a church Jubilation meeting. He was crawling into town like a hound dog who had just had its tail shot off. And the border sweepings he'd ridden out with were no longer with him. In hell by now, Frenchy Belle fervently wished. Her pleasure at seeing Clinton looking all washed-up didn't stop her worrying about the well-being of Mr Brooks and Mr Harding. She hoped just as strongly that they were both OK. She somehow felt that it was so but that could only be wishful thinking on her part. Clinton talking at length to the old man that helped out in the livery barn raised those hopes. Clinton was worrying about something. Frenchy Belle plugged for that something being Mr Brooks and Mr Harding on Clinton's trail again. She walked downstairs and spoke to Jack who was busy filling up the lamps on the lowered hallway chandelier.

'That sonuvabitch, Clinton's back in town, Jack,' she said. 'On his own so it looks like he's met big trouble in Big Creek valley. He could be moving on but I don't think so. Clinton ain't a man that forgets or gives up easily. I think that those two hard-noses, Mr Brooks and Mr Harding are just behind him on the trail so I want you to keep a watch on Clinton, where he's spending his time and, more important, is he hiring more men, savvy?'

'OK, boss,' said Jack. 'I'll stick to him like his shadow. I'll just put my jacket...' But his boss had already left him to dish out some more orders, this time to her girls.

It was late afternoon when Ira reached Two Forks. By switching horses he made a fast, practically non-stop ride. Easy on the horses but bone-aching and tiring for him. He drew up outside the livery barn and dismounted.

'Your two horses are in the corral out back,' the barn owner told Ira. 'Are you intendin' to stay on a spell in Two Forks or do you want my helper to saddle up your horse and use your pard's mount as a packhorse, seeing that he ain't with you?'

Ira gave him a thin-lipped smile. 'Depends,' he said. 'I could be moving out real soon if I don't find what I'm lookin' for. If I find it there could be a fair chance of me staying here for good. And you'll have two extra horses on your hands to sell.'

Ira left the livery barn owner scratching his head in puzzlement over just what the hell did his latest customer mean. Ira hadn't enlightened him any further by telling him that he was looking for the ex-reb guerilla leader, Mr Phil Clinton, so that he could shoot him dead. News of an expected shootout would spread like wildfire, and warn Clinton, if he was in Two Forks, that his tracker had caught up with him. Then it could be that he'd have to look real hard in every side alley in case Clinton was skulking in them hoping to bushwhack him.

A girl he recognized as one of Frenchy Belle's whores grabbed him by the arm. 'Phil Clinton's in town, Mr Brooks,' she said. 'Spending most of his time in the Palace saloon and he's got two men tagging along with him.'

'Thanks for the information, miss,' Ira said. 'But how the hell did you know I was in Two Forks? I've just stepped down from my horse.'

The girl smiled. 'Because you're something special to Miss Frenchy. She saw Clinton ride in, looking she reckoned, that he was being trailed. So we girls have been spelling each other sitting on the front porch waiting for you and Mr Harding to show up. Also, Jack, Miss Frenchy's bouncer, is keeping his eye on Clinton. It was him that told us about the two men. Is Mr Harding OK, Mr

Brooks? Miss Frenchy has sure got herself worrying about the pair of you since Clinton showed his mean face in town. Ain't you goin' to see her first before you go and settle up with Clinton, Mr Brooks?'

Ira's face iced over. 'I ain't lookin' forward to what I'm embarking on, miss, ain't lookin' forward to it one little bit. And it don't help hearing that Clinton's got some backup. But I've worked myself into a fightin' mood and intend calling him out, win or lose.' Face softening he smiled at the girl. 'I sure don't want to lose that feelin' and I would if I paid Miss Frenchy a visit. Why the state I'm in right now I'd fall asleep if I sat in one of her big armchairs and wake up with my blood running cold. And that ain't no condition for a man about to go into a fight. Tell her if things turn out OK for me I'll definitely pay her a visit, a stay awhile visit.'

It was a parched-throated Ira who strode along the boardwalk to the Palace saloon. Without being too cocky he opined that facing Clinton one-to-one he was on a fifty-fifty chance of coming through alive. Three pistols against him changed that view more than somewhat, and it scared the hell out of him, and there could be no backing down. Clinton had to be killed to end once and for all the threat to the valley. Ira thought about all the odds of getting killed he'd faced during the war, Gain's Mill, Manasas, Chancellorsville, with a lot less hope of pulling through in one piece, alive. He gritted his teeth and walked on. He would kill Clinton for sure even if he was drawing his last dying breath.

Clinton was in the Palace when the old man from the livery barn came sidling in by the back entrance. Coming up to Clinton he said, 'There's a fella just pulled in, young, big fella, leading a small remuda, all showing signs of being ridden hard. Don't know if he's one of the fellas you're expectin', Mr Clinton, but he sure wasted no time on the trail from Plainsville.'

Only one of the sons-of-bitches, Clinton

thought. The dynamite must have done for the other sodbuster. Three to one now. Clinton's smile at his informer had a touch of warmth in it. 'You've done well, oldtimer,' he said, and ramming the cork back into his newly opened bottle of whisky he handed it to the old man. 'You go some quiet place and down that, friend.'

The old man clutched the life-saving bottle tightly to his chest and scuttled out of the saloon by the way he'd come in. Clinton walked over to his backup men, playing cards at a nearby table and gave them their orders then he returned to his place at the bar to take up his stance of watching in the bar mirror who came through the swing-doors.

One of the two, city-suited men, sitting at a table at the rear of the saloon, a restless-eyed, hard-faced individual, watched with seemingly casualness the to and froing of the small weasel-faced man at the bar. Noting that one of the card players he had spoken to quickly finished his drink and made his way up the stairs that led to the private rooms.

'I think I've just witnessed a stake-out being set up, Jesse,' he said. 'That weasel-faced bastard at the bar there is expecting trouble soon, shootin' trouble. He's got backup on his left, that black-bearded pilgrim sitting playing cards on his own and there's another fella just went upstairs, and he ain't gone up there for pleasure. I can see him layin' back up against the wall, ideally placed for a drop shot on some poor, unsuspecting sonuvabitch.'

Jesse grinned at his brother. 'So long as it ain't us he's setting a trap for, Frank, that's all that matters. Drink up and relax.'

'Mr Brooks?' Ira's hand dropped nervously to the butt of his pistol as he close-eyed the man sitting on the edge of the boardwalk who had spoken his name.

'Yeah, that's me,' Ira replied. 'Who's doin' the askin'?'

Still gazing across the street the man said, 'I'm Jack Purdie, work for Frenchy Belle.

I've been keepin' an eye on your friend Clinton for her. Though by you being headin' for the Palace I reckon one of the girls will have told you the setup in there, Clinton hirin' himself two guns to back him up. But you ain't heard the worst, Mr Brooks, the asshole knows you're in town and seeking him out. You'll be walking into a trap. There's a man upstairs and another at a table to the left of the bar. I'll come in with you being that your pard ain't with you just to even up the odds a mite in your favour.'

'No need to, Mr Purdie,' Ira said. 'It ain't your fight but I'm obliged all the same, and thanks for putting me in the picture. I'm owin' to you and the girls, and Frenchy Belle. There is one more thing you can do for me, Mr Purdie.'

'Name it, Mr Brooks,' Purdie said. 'Frenchy Belle gave me orders to help you all I could.'

'What the hell does Clinton look like?' Ira blurted out. 'I ain't seen the sonuvabitch in daylight. And I've only been told what he looks like.'

'Sweet Jesus,' Purdie breathed, and twisting round, looked up at Ira. 'You sure do like to do things the hard way, Mr Brooks. Clinton's a thin-built squirt of a man, wears Johnny Reb pants and a store-cut jacket, favours wearing his gun on his left side, in a cavalry holster.' Purdie got to his feet. 'Here, take this,' he pressed a small pistol into Ira's hand. 'You might sneak a few seconds on Clinton with it. He won't see it in your hand and if you get close enough that little beauty will fell a steer. I can't help you with the two backups though. You'll have to come up with some real fancy shootin' to get the drop on them. Good luck. Mr Brooks, I'll wait out here to see how you fare. Frenchy Belle will want to know, either way.'

Ira looked at the Derringer in his hand. He wasn't fooled by its smallness. The .41 balls were real man-downers. 'Thanks, Mr Purdie,' he said and cocking both barrels he closed his fingers over the pistol and continued on his way to the Palace saloon.

As he stepped through the swing doors Ira struggled to keep his gaze from honing in on the top of the stairs, seeking out one of the backups. Better, he thought, to keep Clinton innocent of the fact that he knew he was walking into a trap. Clinton would have to be downed first. Mr Purdie's hideaway gun was the weapon to do that if Clinton let him get close in. Next would be the man upstairs. The other man at the table was a bigger problem. Then, Ira thought that it was no good getting himself in a sweat trying to work things out that far ahead. Clinton could down him first.

Clinton saw Ira come into the saloon through the mirror and slid his hand between his belly and the bar counter, gripping the butt of the pistol he had taken out of its holster and slipped it in the top of his pants. Noting that Ira's gun hand was well clear of his pistol he let him come a few paces closer for a real killing shot, then wolf-smiling, he spun round, heaving his pistol out. Ira saw a man turning fast in his direction, glimpsed the sheen of a fisted gun. He didn't look to see if the man wore Confederate army pants, his hair-trigger nerves acted automatically, pumping off both loads of the Derringer for him. Clinton bounced back against the bar as the two balls hit him in the chest. Ira thought that Clinton had the look of a man who knew he was mortally wounded but he had no more time to spend finding out for sure, he was down on one knee, drawing out his Colt to take on the gunman on the balcony. Bitterly knowing that it would be too late, the man was at the railings aiming down at him.

The noise of two shots ringing out behind him made Ira's flesh cringe as though he had been hit. To his surprise the man on the balcony keeled over backwards, vanishing from his view. He straightened up, his face a wild, frightened grimace, and looked behind him. Two men, dude-dressed, were sheathing pistols in shoulder holsters. To their left, in an untidy heap of upturned chairs, lay Clinton's second backup man. As still and as dead as he now knew Clinton was. Ira heard the older of the two men say, 'It's all over, gents. Those three dead and departed sonsuvbitches tried to cut the kid down. We only tried to make it a fair fight.' Frank nodded to Ira then he and Jesse walked out of the saloon. A slightly less nerve-jumping Ira sheathed his gun and followed them out, leaving behind a babble of voices as the drinkers began to discuss the shooting that had lightened up a dull afternoon's drinking.

Ira caught up with his saviours on the boardwalk. 'I'd like to thank you gents,' he said. 'Not many men would draw their guns to prevent a stranger from getting his foolish head blown off. I'm beholden to you both.'

'We were only payin' a debt off, isn't that so, Jesse?' Frank replied.

'We sure were, Frank,' replied Jesse. Grinning at Ira he said, 'We met a while back, across in Missouri, on the Lexington turnpike, remember? You put us on to a bunch of no-good Yankees who were aimin' to bushwhack us. So as Frank said, we owed you.'

'Yeah, I remember now,' Ira said. 'And your debt you thought you owed me has been settled.' And thanked God for his meeting them on the trail that day.

'We'll be moving on, mister,' said Frank. 'It's been nice to have been of some assistance to you.'

Purdie joined him as he watched the pair head towards the livery barn. 'You've got some real hard-nosed friends, Mr Brooks,' he said. 'Those are the James boys, got prices on their heads in Clay County, Missouri.'

'Mr Purdie,' a serious-voiced Ira said. 'I would have welcomed the Devil himself giving me a hand in there, and that's a fact. Now I made a promise that I would pay Frenchy Belle a long call the next time I came here but if I don't ride back to Big Creek valley Mr Harding will be ass-kickin' it to Two Forks to see if I'm OK. And he's got a busted shoulder to contend with, also he's sparkin' up to a widow woman, so he don't want to be wasting his time on the trail.'

Frenchy Belle had been told by Lisa that Ira was in town. Then she saw him herself talking to Purdie before going into the saloon. She heard the sound of gunfire and the waiting to see who would come out of the saloon made her grip the balcony rail so hard her knuckles whitened under the strain. She swayed unsteadily with relief when Ira stepped into the street. She began to wonder if Mr Brooks would, as he'd said, stay on a while in Two Forks now that the trouble was over. He seemed a man of his word. Though in her lifetime of dealing with men she had found that most of them would lie their socks off if it suited their purpose.

'So you see, Miss Frenchy,' Ira said, 'why I must ride back to the valley. They'll still be standing to arms there, wondering if me or Clinton's dead. But I'll be back. What I've got left there won't hurt stayin' as it is for a while longer.'

Frenchy Belle accepted Ira's reason for returning to the valley. Hiding her disappointment she smiled and said, 'You do that, Mr Brooks, come back here, I'll be waiting, as long as you're not hard-assin' after another bunch of owlhoots.'

Frenchy Belle spent the most of the third day since Ira had left on her balcony waiting anxiously for signs of his return. She wasn't expecting, or needing, a boy meets girl story book romance thing. She was well past that bunkum. But she did have the craving to be treated like a real lady and not as the whorehouse madam she was, for a few days at least. Why? She couldn't explain to herself why. Must be her age. One thing she was sure of, Mr Ira Brooks could supply that need. She smiled. The hard-nose sodbuster was sure playing hard to get. Suddenly Frenchy Belle stopped her ruminating as she saw the trail-dust of a single rider along the

Plainsville trail. 'Good Lord!' she gasped. She wasn't dressed to meet him. She dashed back indoors.

When Ira came out of the livery barn Frenchy Belle was standing on her balcony dressed in the same see-through clothes she was wearing when he had first seen her.

Frenchy Belle, not caring a damn what her girls would think of her, shouted to Ira as he was crossing the street. 'Am I still as purty, Mr Brooks?'

A grinning Ira took off his hat in a sweeping gesture and bent at the middle in an "honour your partner bow". 'Every bit, ma'am, every bit!'

Still raising her voice, Frenchy Belle said, 'Well don't hang about there in the street like a country boy that's lost his nerve. Come on in the whorehouse you sonuvabitch! You've kept me danglin' long enough!' Her beaming smile belied the shouted anger in her voice.

The publishers hope that this book has given you enjoyable reading. Large Print Books are especially designed to be as easy to see and hold as possible. If you wish a complete list of our books please ask at your local library or write directly to:

Dales Large Print Books
Magna House, Long Preston,
Skipton, North Yorkshire.
BD23 4ND